A Governess for the Icy Viscount

A Clean Regency Romance Novel

Emily Barnet

Copyright © 2024 by Emily Barnet
All Rights Reserved.
This book may not be reproduced or transmitted in any form without the written permission of the publisher. In no way is it legal to reproduce, duplicate, or transmit any part of this document in either electronic means or in printed format. Recording of this publication is strictly prohibited and any storage of this document is not allowed unless with written permission from the publisher.

Table of Contents

Prologue 4
Chapter One 11
Chapter Two 18
Chapter Three 24
Chapter Four 33
Chapter Five 40
Chapter Six 47
Chapter Seven 55
Chapter Eight 62
Chapter Nine 71
Chapter Ten 77
Chapter Eleven 85
Chapter Twelve 92
Chapter Thirteen 97
Chapter Fourteen 104
Chapter Fifteen 111
Chapter Sixteen 118
Chapter Seventeen 124
Chapter Eighteen 131
Chapter Nineteen 139
Chapter Twenty 146
Chapter Twenty-one 152
Chapter Twenty-two 160
Chapter Twenty-three 166
Chapter Twenty-four 174
Chapter Twenty-five 180

Epilogue 186
Extended Epilogue 192

Prologue

Three years prior

Julian Rollins waited outside the bedchamber of his wife and viscountess, Eliza, wearing out the floorboards of the polished mahogany floor as he walked back and forth with his hands clasped behind his back and chewed on his bottom lip. Their third child was on the way, and he was both thrilled and nervous.

Through the thick door, he could hear urgent, dampened whispers of the physician and the midwife, though he could not hear what they were saying. Each minute that passed felt like its own eternity, just as it had with their previous two children. Yet Julian could not escape the mounting trepidation that crept into his mind. Had it taken so long with Henry and Elizabeth?

To keep himself occupied, he turned his chaotic thoughts to what the future would bring for his growing family. He and Eliza adored each other, as much as any noble couple in the ton had ever loved one another. They had welcomed both their children, six-year-old Henry, and four-year-old Elizabeth, with overflowing joy and love.

In the years since Elizabeth's birth, Julian had believed he could not be happier. But with the arrival of their third child, Julian's heart was ready to burst. Both their older children were thrilled to have a little brother or sister. And Julian hoped there would be many more additions to their loving, wonderful family. He had his heir, which was vital to his family's legacy. But he had found that being a father, apart from being a husband, was his favorite and most important role of all.

He smiled as he imagined himself holding the tiny infant in his arms. He pictured the face of his dearly beloved Eliza, tired from the laborious task of birthing their third little miracle but lit with the radiant glow of happiness at welcoming another perfect child into their household, smiling up at him with all the love in the world in her eyes. He pictured the two of them sharing the sweet kiss that only those riding the rush of renewed parenthood could.

Despite the gnawing worry, he smiled to himself. Everything is perfectly fine, he assured himself. Dr. Brown is a commendable physician, and Eliza is a strong woman. Mother will be out any moment now to tell me that it is time to see my new baby.

As he allowed the thoughts to take root in his mind and grant him comfort, the door to his wife's bedchambers opened slowly behind him. He whirled around to see that Augusta Rollins was indeed exiting the room. He rushed over to his mother with eager anticipation. But the smile faltered on his lips as he looked down into his mother's pale, ashen face, and tear-filled eyes.

"Mother?" he asked, putting a gentle hand on her shoulder. "Pray tell, what ails you?"

The dowager viscountess shook her head, not speaking for nearly a full minute.

"Julian, darling," she said, her voice trembling and filled with heartbreak. "I am so very sorry."

Julian shook his head, not understanding. Or perhaps, he did not want to understand.

"Mother, what is it?" he asked. "How are Eliza and the infant faring?"

His mother took a moment to wipe tears from her cheeks and take a deep, trembling breath.

"They are gone, Julian," she said. "There was a terrible complication. Dr. Brown did everything he could. But there was so much blood... We lost them both, sweetheart."

Julian shook his head once more, firmly, as though he could erase his mother's words and make them untrue.

"I do not understand," he said. "Eliza is healthy. The baby is strong. There should not be any complications."

The dowager put a hand on her son's shoulder and looked at him with sorrowful eyes.

"I am so sorry, darling," she said.

Julian felt his entire world tilt. The edges of his vision turned black, and he held onto his mother to maintain his balance. Could what his mother was saying be true? Was there some cruel twist that had allowed him to mishear her?

"No," he whispered, willing the universe to correct itself and realize it had made a terrible mistake. But when the physician came out of the room, carrying his medical bag in his arms and wearing an expression identical to that of the dowager's, Julian choked.

Dr. Brown approached him hesitantly, patting him firmly on the back.

"I am so very sorry for your loss, Lord Rollins," he said. He continued speaking, but Julian could not hear a word. He opened his mouth to argue with the physician, to order him back inside the bedchambers and save his wife and child. But no sound came out. At least, he did not hear any sound.

He was unaware that he had been screaming unintelligible gibberish until his mother wrapped her arms tightly around him, holding her close to him and sobbing. Then, the sound returned to the world, and his screams reverberated throughout the entirety of Rollins Manor.

Julian drew in a painful breath, his throat raw and growing hoarse. He tried to enter the bedchambers to see for himself, desperate for any way that he might prove Dr. Brown and his mother wrong. But the dowager grabbed onto him once more, surprisingly strong in her grip.

"Darling, do not go in there," she said. "It will haunt you for the rest of your life."

Julian's heart was shattered. He did not think that seeing his wife one last time, no matter in what state, would be any more haunting than the fact that he would never see her again after that day. But the numbness of shock that had kept him on his feet was giving way to the crushing grief that he knew would burden him for the rest of his days, making him weak and unsteady on his feet.

He staggered backward, falling away from his mother, and tumbling torso into the banister that separated the second floor of the manor from the first. His mind was reeling. Just that morning, he and Eliza had awoken, filled with joy and future plans. Now, the life the two of them had built with such care and delight was forever changed.

Julian did not feel either his valet, Alexander, or his butler,

Wyatt, come running to his aid. They flanked him, grabbing onto each arm and turning him away from the banister. It was only as they were pulling him toward his chambers that he understood they had likely saved him from a horrible accident. *I wish they had let me fall*, he thought with a numb bitterness that would become too familiar to him.

Alexander took it upon himself to dismiss the butler when they reached Julian's bedchambers. Wyatt bowed, but Julian hardly noticed. Alexander had to drag Julian, who felt as though all his limbs had become completely paralyzed, to the bed. The valet gently undressed his master, helping him into his night dress. But Julian offered no aid. He sat like a child's doll, only moving with the assistance of the puppeteer and utterly useless otherwise.

"Milord," Alexander said as he gathered up Julian's clothes. "May I provide you with anything?"

Julian shook his head, amazed that it felt so heavy, as if it had been replaced by a bag of wet sand.

"No," he said.

Alexander's brow furrowed.

"Lord Rollins, you must eat," he said. His warm, gray eyes were filled with concern. But Julian merely shook his head once more.

"No," he said, doubting that he would ever eat again.

The question was repeated thrice more, and Julian's response was identical twice. The third time, he sat staring through the wall in front of him, feeling his reason and sanity balancing on a tenuous rope.

At last, Alexander exited, leaving Julian alone with his thoughts. Immediately, the images he had concocted as he had waited for Eliza to deliver their unborn child flooded his mind. Eliza's smile, the face of their sleeping newborn, a kiss and a shared bonding moment with his wife and newest child all haunted him now as though their ghosts had taken up residence in his mind. He did not remember lying down on his bed or falling asleep. But when he awoke, he was screaming Eliza's name at the top of his voice.

For the next week, Julian did not open the door to his

chambers. He ignored every knock and every plea for him to either come out or let someone in. He lay in bed for the first four of those days, staring at the white canopy above during the merciless hours when sleep would not allow him reprieve. His sleep was without nightmares, and he supposed he could thank his mother for that. Had she not stopped him from entering Eliza's chambers that day, his dreams might have tortured him into illness.

However, his sleep was not dreamless. The true torment lay in the dreams where he was waiting outside Eliza's door and the physician came out smiling, delivering the news to Julian that he and his wife had twins, or sometimes, triplets. He could hear every sound, smell every scent, and feel the soft, downy skin of his newborn babies' cheeks beneath his fingertips when he touched them. Waking from those dreams was like losing them all over again, and the agony and rage compounded each time.

On the eighth day after Eliza's horrific passing, Julian's attention was drawn to a sliding sound against the wood floors of his chambers. He looked up to see an envelope coming to a stop just beyond the threshold of the door. He listened, waiting either for a knock or for the sound of retreating footsteps. After a brief pause, he heard the latter, and he cautiously pulled himself out of bed. He grabbed the letter, opening it and casting aside the ripped envelope. He opened it, and for the first time in over a week, he almost smiled.

Dearest Brother,

    I just received Mother's letter about what has happened. I cannot tell you how sorry I am for your great loss, and no words could ever adequately express how my heart breaks for you and your family. I wish to send you all my love, and my deepest condolences in your time of grief. I apologise that I cannot be there with you now, as I am still away on business. But I shall return in one week, and my first priority is to come and see you.

    I understand that your pain must be great now, and I can only imagine how difficult it must be to think about the future. But do not allow it to consume you. Let your duties and work offer you aid during this time. It would grieve me to see you wither into insignificance, wasting away in grief that could easily claim your life, as well. Please, Brother. Eliza would never wish to see your pain swallow you. And please, know that if you ever need, I will be right there for you. You need only ask.

    All my love,
    George

Julian read his younger brother's letter with tears in his eyes. He knew there was no way that his mother could have told George about his days in bed, not when he was so far away. In the days since Eliza's death, it felt like George was the only one who understood Julian's agony.

And Julian also understood something. His younger brother was right; the grief was, indeed, consuming him. It would be difficult to find any heart to care about business affairs or his duties as viscount. But if he built walls around his wounded heart, he might be able to carry on, if only as a specter of his former self.

And in the following days, Julian did precisely that. He retreated into his study, and further into himself, shutting out his staff, his mother and even his two surviving children. He forced himself to focus on ledgers and letters to business partners, thinking of nothing but work and his responsibilities as Viscount Rollins from dawn until dusk.

He ignored the stark coldness that settled within the once warm, lively walls of Rollins Manor, even as it began to mirror the dying warmth in his own heart. His one place of solace became his study, and silence became the only sound he wanted to hear. If he could not have the family he wanted, he would have nothing to do with anyone else at all.

Chapter One

Present day

Sophia Hartley sat at a worn oak table, studying the half-finished blue dress in front of her with great care. She squinted through the dim lighting that streamed in through the small window of the equally small dining room of the modest London apartment she shared with her mother and sister. Her fingers worked a needle and thread through the linen fabric with adept skill, weaving through the seams with the precision only years of practice could yield.

Beside her, twelve-year-old Lucy worked on mending a scarf that matched the blue dress. The scarf was a simpler task, which Sophia had had no problem delegating to her younger sister. She easily could have done it, true enough. But it was time that Lucy learned how to sew and crochet. Their family depended on having another set of hands that could take on work, however small.

The matriarch of their family, Mrs. Caroline Hartley, sat at the head of the small, tired table, staring at a pair of trousers. They were finery, commissioned by a wealthy merchant. Mr. Thomas George with whom Sophia and Lucy's father, Dennis, often did business. He had been one of their regular customers since Dennis Hartley died eighteen months prior due to consumption. But even his custom came less and less in recent months, as he was approaching retirement.

Sophia glanced up as her mother's brow furrowed. The dark circles beneath her dull blue eyes spoke of many late nights working on what little mending jobs they could get. And the gray streaks that had appeared over the past half a year spoke of a grieving widow who was struggling more each week to provide for her two daughters. The worry and fatigue never left her mother's eyes, and Sophia did not know how much longer she could sustain their family on their meager income.

Father's medical bills alone could send us to the poorhouse,

Sophia thought as her fingers moved faster to finish the dress before sundown. The woman who hired them said she would be back to retrieve her dress and scarf before supper that evening, and they needed that money so Caroline could go to the market and buy more food. We truly believed the physician could get Father well. Yet even with his passing, the doctor shows no mercy.

She shook off the thought before it could begin forming bitterness in her mind. The physician had taken the best care he could of her father during the three weeks he lasted with the illness but their money was already drastically diminished due to some poor business decisions her father made two months before he fell ill.

They had paid every coin in their savings for treatment, but Dennis Hartley only became more ill by the day. It was not the doctor's fault, and he deserved to be paid for services he rendered to Sophia's family on credit. But was there not a way to work off some of the debt, rather than to hand over money that was already running dangerously low?

She shook her head once more. She was being unreasonable. And she was aware of it. She knew that she could not let the worry and frustration lead her to such thoughts. Besides, she knew very well that her sister and mother depended on her strength and endurance. It would not do to allow them to perceive her entertaining such nonsensical notions.

She missed her father, with her entire heart but the debts he had left behind, which seemed to compound by the hour, were a large burden. She also knew that her mother and sister missed Dennis, as well. And they were just as weighted by the financial bind in which her father's debts had left them. She had no right to allow selfish thoughts to enter her mind. She needed to find a more substantial way to help provide for her family and herself.

That night, she lay awake as Lucy slept soundly in the small straw cot beside hers. She stared at the ceiling, which was beginning to crack, trying to think of practical solutions for their money troubles. She could try taking on more sewing work. But there was only so much work to be had for the three Hartley women. More people were taking their mending to bona fide seamstresses in downtown, or simply buying more clothes. She had to admit to herself that soon enough, there would likely be next to no work for them.

Oh, how I miss you, Father, she thought, covering her mouth to stifle a sob. I wish you were here. I wish you could help me find a way to care for Mother and Lucy.

Then, an idea struck her. There were people within the ton who had acquaintances who helped women find suitable positions within wealthy, noble households. The newspaper office would be a place where they might have information of a job available. London abounded with women of diverse backgrounds whose husbands had passed away, leaving them to fend for themselves and their children, with scant provision for the future.

She had never spoken with any such people, but she had heard women just a couple years younger than her talking about how they ended up with positions as maids, governesses, cooks and nursemaids, even at such young ages. Surely, a woman with her education could find some luck with an acquaintance like that. She decided, as her eyelids finally grew heavy, that she would rise early the next morning and go speak with one.

***

Just as the sky was beginning to lighten, Sophia slipped out of bed, quietly fetching the one clean dress she had, a pale blue cotton dress with matching boots and gloves that she had sewn herself and pulling it over her. She styled her hair into a neat bun, then put on her boots and gloves. As quietly as she could manage, she sneaked out of the apartment, hurrying to the road and heading for the city centre. The walk would take about an hour, but Sophia was still quite early setting out, and she thought she could use the fresh air.

London was a different place during the quiet hours of early morning. Shop keepers were just entering their businesses, making muffled noises as they cleaned and prepared for the day. The voices of the other few pedestrians she saw were subdued, as though they were trying to keep from waking their sleepy city. And with the streets not crowded by carriages and buggies, the tall buildings and sleek storefronts looked like regal sentinels against the bright morning London sky.

She reached the newspaper office just as she saw a young lady unlock the door and step back inside. She paused as she reached the building, smoothing out the skirt of her dress and tucking a stray clump of hair back into her bun. She looked presentable, even with as poor as her family was. She just hoped she was presentable enough.

She entered the office, her breath catching as she looked around. The large, rounded reception desk, small tables and yellow floral upholstered chairs were made from Rosewood. The upholstery itself was a luxurious batiste fabric, and the rose and lily patterns on the yellow material made Sophia think of the first blooms of spring. It was clearly a well-established and profitable business to have such magnificent furnishings.

"I am Mrs. Abernathy," a sharp, stern voice said. "May I help you?"

Sophia whirled around, trying not to appear as startled as she was. She locked eyes with a lanky, strict-looking woman who was dressed in a professional, brown muslin dress. Her mousy brown hair was pulled back in a bun so tight that Sophia thought it lifted her eyebrows. Her thin nose was wrinkled as though she smelled something sour, and her ice blue eyes were narrowed, appearing to glare straight into Sophia's soul.

Sophia tried to shake off the intimidation with which the woman filled her. She returned the stark greeting with a warm smile as she approached the desk.

"Good morning," she said, her nerves vibrating her entire body. "My name is Sophia Hartley, and I would like to know about any governess positions you might know of through your acquaintances."

The woman looked her over as though she already knew that Sophia did not have any experience as a governess. Or as anything besides a mediocre seamstress, she thought, flushing as the errant thought filled her with shame. She needed to focus. And she would have to hope that her education and gentle demeanor would be enough to secure employment.

"Where are your references?" Mrs. Abernathy asked, looking pointedly at Sophia's empty, clasped hands.

Sophia forced herself to concentrate, giving the stern woman a bright smile.

"I have worked as a seamstress with my mother for the past few years," she said. "Thus, I do not have any experience as a governess. However, I am well educated, and I love children. My sister is twelve, and I have greatly enjoyed watching her grow into a young lady."

The matron sneered at her, the disapproval so apparent on her face that Sophia was sure that even a passersby across the street could see it.

"I am sure you have developed incredible skills, working with your mother as your employer," she said, the sarcasm thick and jagged. "However, that is hardly something you could use as a reference. And your sister would be your mother's charge, just as you were. Not yours. I do not think you understand the challenges of being a governess, or what noblemen and women expect from women who fulfill that role."

Sophia nodded, even though she was acutely aware that she did not understand those things.

"I know that caring for children is a tremendous responsibility," she said. "And nothing is more important to me than education, especially for every child. I have helped my sister with her lessons since she was..."

"As I told you, your sister was not your charge," Mrs. Abernathy said, cutting her off so sharply that she winced. "I am sure that you taught your sister well. But that is not something you can put as a reference."

Sophia nodded again, losing the heart to defend herself. She needed the work, and she knew that governess positions paid well and typically included long tenures for the women who could prove themselves.

Seeming satisfied with Sophia's silence, Mrs. Abernathy smirked.

"You can ask people as many times over," she said.

"However, if you do not have any experience or references, it will be next to impossible for any of us to place you in a position. And then, there is the matter of vacancies for governess. Which, I regret to inform you, we do not currently have. I will add your name to the waiting list. But with your lack of references, you will almost certainly be overlooked for women with credible experience."

Sophia's heart sank. She knew there were other places she could ask in London. But she also knew that they would probably say various versions of what Mrs. Abernathy had just told her. The slim hope with which she had entered the newspaper office dissolved, leaving her feeling deflated and more worried than ever before.

Dejected, she slowly made her way back to her family's apartment. Her stomach twisted as she glanced up at the building and noticed the tattered curtains fluttering in the window of the living area. She put on a smile, grateful that she had not told her mother or sister what she was planning. She could suffer the disappointment of rejection. But she didn't want them to have to cope with it, as well.

She entered the dining area of the small apartment just as her mother was setting their only pot in the middle of the table. Her mother gave her a tired smile and gestured to her seat.

"There you are," she said. "I was beginning to worry that you would not make it home in time for lunch."

Sophia forced her smile to widen as Lucy bound into the room. Sophia was glad that her younger sister could still find joy, even in their meager life. But it added to the guilt of her failure.

As the three women ate in silence, Sophia bit back tears. Watching her mother and sister eat their insufficient portions of celery stew and stale bread reminded her that their finances were only going to worsen, rather than improve. Sophia herself could not eat her share as she could not stop thinking about how critical it was that she find some way to secure something like a governess position. She silently promised herself to pour her meal back into the pot so that her mother and sister would have an extra serving for their next meal.

After lunch, their mother excused Lucy to go finish her lessons, while Sophia followed her into the conjoined kitchen to help her clean up. Mrs. Hartley scrubbed the dishes while Sophia rinsed them. It took a few minutes for Sophia to gather her nerve. Once she could bring herself to speak, she paused her work and turned to her mother.

"I went to seek for a job as governess today, Mother," she said.

Mrs. Hartley looked at her eldest daughter with a tired hopefulness that made Sophia second guess mentioning her failed attempt to the frail woman.

"Oh, darling, that is wonderful," she said.

Sophia shook her head, looking at her mother with apologetic eyes.

"It was not, I am afraid," she said, explaining everything that Mrs. Abernathy had said to her.

Her mother gave her another tired smile, and Sophia's heart ached as the brief flicker of hope in her eyes melted into the same worry and disappointment that had lingered in her gaze since her husband's death.

"Sweetheart, you will not always succeed the very first time you try something," she said. "I am proud of you simply for trying. And I know that you will have better luck in the future. You are a very smart and clever young woman, and you are the kindest and most patient person I know. Furthermore you are quite determined. You must not let one rejection shape your ideas for the future."

Sophia smiled at her mother, desperate to find comfort in her mother's words. She knew there was a chance that she would be more successful in her future endeavors to find work. However, she also knew it was equally possible that she would not be; not the next time she tried to apply, or the next time, or the next. And the uncertainty was scarier than all the obstacles that she and her family had faced since her father's death combined.

Chapter Two

Three years to the day after Eliza died, Julian sat in melancholy silence at his desk in his study. Across from him hung the portrait of his late wife, and he stared with longing eyes at her beautiful porcelain face, framed by shiny, dark brown hair. The painting hardly did justice to the sheen of her ringlets and the sparkle in her bright hazel eyes. But on the anniversary of her passing, he knew it was as close as he would ever get to seeing his beloved Eliza ever again.

His heart ached as he gazed up at her image. Well-wishers and loved ones had assured him that time would ease the agony he felt. But even years later, the pain was still as fresh and intense as it had been on the day he lost her forever. Worse still, his duties as viscount did not care about the gut-wrenching grief in his heart. They awaited him and demanded his attention, even on the days when the pain was so great that he could hardly pull himself from his bed.

Eliza, my love, how I miss you, he thought, grunting as tears stung his eyes. The only way I can survive, albeit barely, is to envision you holding our sweet little baby in your arms, smiling down on me.

On all of you, Eliza's soft, sweet voice chastised him in her gentle, loving tone.

Julian sighed. Of course, he had not forgotten their two surviving children since her passing. However, he had kept a careful distance from them. In Henry, he saw Eliza's eyes, so brilliant and hazel and filled with insatiable curiosity. And in Elizabeth, he saw Eliza's every feature, down to the dimple in her chin. He loved his children, to be sure. But seeing their faces reminded him of the woman he would never again hold. He had to keep them away from him, lest they begin thinking he blamed them for the loss of their mother. And for the sake of his own sanity.

He was in the midst of justifying his strategic detachment

from his children when there was a knock on the door.

"Come," he said, rubbing his eyes in frustration. He resented the interruption. But when he saw it was his mother, he softened, if only a little.

The dowager viscountess approached her son with her hands clasped firmly at her bosom. Her mouth was pulled tight, and her eyes were filled with concern. Julian did his best to collect his expression, trying to pretend as though he had been studying a document on his desk. He motioned for the dowager to sit across from him, which she did.

"Julian, I come with grave news," she said.

Julian closed his eyes and took a slow, deep breath.

"What is it, Mother?" he asked.

Augusta sighed.

"It is the governess," she said. "She has unexpectedly resigned, citing her father's illness as her cause for such sudden employment termination."

Julian stared at his mother. Although it was far from the best news she could have given to him, it was also far from the worst. Had she needed to disrupt his brooding solitude for that?

"Could this matter not have waited until the morning?" he asked. His frigid demeanor was tempered, but barely. He wanted to be left to his thoughts again, not deal with the petty dealings of the household.

The dowager shook her head, surveying Julian.

"I am afraid not, Julian," she said. Her tone took on a slight edge of defensiveness. "This impacts the children, leaving them without the care and education they require. Every moment is of the essence."

Julian sighed.

"I will write a letter to be posted to the newspaper tomorrow," he said. "That is the best I can do, as I am already behind in my ledgers." His mother did not speak or move to leave the study. She stood, still staring at him, until he spoke again. "Is there something else, Mother?"

The dowager took a deep breath, straightening her shoulders. Julian braced himself. This was clearly a discussion she was prepared to have until she was completely satisfied with Julian's response. Still, he waited to hear what she was about to say.

"I am concerned for the well-being of Elizabeth and Henry," she said. "They need someone to care for them immediately."

Julian nodded with deliberate slowness.

"That is why we have household staff, is it not?" he asked. "And as I have already said, I shall write to the newspaper tomorrow and call for a new governess."

His mother sighed, but she remained where she was.

"I believe that they need more than a governess, darling," she said.

Julian raised an eyebrow, his defenses rising.

"What do you mean?" he asked warily, not liking the calculation in his mother's eyes.

The dowager sighed.

"They need education, to be sure," she said. "However, they also need a mother figure in their lives. Especially with their father so busy with duties and business."

Julian tightened his jaw, locking a firm gaze with his mother. Her implication, and the entire reason for her disturbing him in his study, was suddenly abundantly clear.

"This is not something I am prepared to discuss, Mother," he said, freezing the words with his tone. "Now, if you will excuse me."

The dowager shook her head, her own gaze intensifying.

"You must consider remarrying," she said, dropping her previous charade of being concerned about the children's education and getting straight to her true point. "Henry and Elizabeth are young enough right now to still gain a positive effect on their lives if you take another wife. But I fear that if you wait too long, it will be too late.

Julian stood from his chair with such force and speed that his chair slammed into the cabinets behind him. Grief mixed with anger, coursing through him as though attached to racehorses.

"Remarriage is out of the question," he said. "I have made that clear enough since her death. I have no intention of replacing

Eliza in the children's or my life. I have already refused to replace her in our hearts. And I will not tell you this again. Leave the subject at this, Mother. I shall not be discussing it with you again."

The dowager pursed her lips, and Julian understood that his words carried little weight with her. His rage simmered in his blood, and he braced himself for what he was sure would be a bitter argument. There was a long pause, and Julian wished that she would simply leave the table, and the subject, altogether.

"Julian, I understand your grief over Eliza," she said. "I loved her like a daughter. And losing your father allows me to share in the ache left in the hearts of widows and widowers when a spouse dies. But there are more important things at stake here, and I do not think you understand that."

Julian's skin prickled as his anger flexed within him.

"If you understand, then what do you feel could be so important that it is worth trampling the death and loss of such dearly loved ones?" he asked.

The dowager threw up her hands, as though she herself was growing frustrated. She shook her head, looking exasperated.

"The children, Julian," she said.

Julian nodded, biting down on his back molars to keep from losing his temper.

"I believe we just addressed the children," he said. "I told you that there will be no woman who replaces their mother. There is no more to discuss on the subject. As for their education, we shall find someone to fill the role of governess. That is all that relates to the children, Mother."

Augusta shook her head and furrowed her brow.

"You alone cannot make a stable home and life for them," she said. "I should not need to tell you how important it is that they have a mother figure in their lives, and that they have security in their household. I understand that you may never love another as you loved Eliza. But this is not just about you. You must think of what is best for the children."

Julian shook his head, his nostrils flaring as he tried once more to get his mother to leave the discussion alone.

"I am thinking of what is best for them," he said. "They will get a nurturing woman as governess, and they have a nursemaid. They do not need a new mother. Not when their dead one was so well loved."

The dowager regarded Julian with all the vexation of a jaded phaeton driver.

"How can you say that is what is best for them, when they are starved for affection?" she asked.

Julian had had enough. He pointed toward the study door, his eyes sending the message that he was more than done with the topic.

"Leave, Mother," he said, pounding his fist on the desk, struggling to keep control over the volume of his voice. "I will not discuss this with you further. Not now, and not ever again. Is that clear?"

The dowager stared at her son, clearly shocked. Julian knew he was coming across very abrasively, and he knew he needed to calm himself. But he also wanted to ensure that his mother knew that he would not tolerate her pushing him about marriage. No matter her intent, as he had told her, he would never even consider replacing Eliza. And that was final.

At last, Augusta turned on her heel and marched out of the study. Julian waited until the door closed behind her, which did so with considerable force. Then, he settled back into his chair, sighing deeply. He put his head in his hands as he battled with the feelings his mother had stirred. He had made his entire life about fulfilling each of his duties as viscount. Now, his mother had placed one more onto him, one which he had already fulfilled once when he married Eliza. How could he ever consider fulfilling it again?

With a deep breath, Julian rose once more. He opened the study door, calling for Wyatt. The butler appeared less than a minute later, bowing respectfully to his master.

"I require you to see to contacting the people at the newspaper office immediately," he said. "It is of the utmost urgency that we replace the governess we just lost. The children cannot be without critical education at such impressionable ages. Nothing takes priority over this task, is that clear?"

Wyatt bowed, giving Julian another smile.

23

"I understand, milord," he said.

Julian nodded, dismissing the butler with a wave of his hand. When Wyatt was gone, he went back to his desk, his eyes landing on the portrait of his late wife once more.

Darling, what do I do? He pleaded silently. Eliza had once been his grounded center. He could go to her for any advice, and she always knew just what to say. He tried to think of what she might say to him right then. But as it happened more often of late, her voice, and her words, were forgotten.

Deep down, he knew what his decision would be. It did not matter what society or his duties demanded of him. He was unable to allow another bride into his life. He had told his mother that the children would have a new governess to fulfill the role of a feminine influence in their lives, as well as their ensured guarantee of getting the education they needed. And he had meant those words. He was, in fact, prioritizing his children's needs, as his mother had mentioned. But why did their needs have to include him inviting another woman into their lives in any sense other than that of an employee?

Chapter Three

In the two days following her trip to the newspaper office, Sophia had spent her time vying for extra customers for her mother, sister, and her, trying not to think about what the woman at the office had said to her about her lack of experience and references.

If she was a dishonest woman, she might have invented references who had, since the termination of imaginary employment, set sail for France or the Far East. She was not a dishonest woman, however, and thus, she had applied with exactly what she had, which was nothing.

Still, as she sat in the living room of their small apartment, mending a skirt with meticulous diligence, she wondered if she should not have found some way to make herself sound a little more experienced than she was. Could she have included tending to her mother's younger offspring, considering the sizable age gap of eight years between them? What about the times she had looked after Mrs. Smith's twin five-year-old girls when she went to market?

No, she thought, scolding herself. They meant experience with tutoring children professionally. Not relatives or as favours for a neighbour.

With a sigh, she tried to push aside her thoughts. There was nothing for it now. She had already turned in her application, and she had done it the only moral way to do it. She would not want to earn a job with dishonesty because that would not truly be earning it.

Besides, it might take the job away from a hard-working, honest governess who was struggling even more than she and her own family were. No. She would just have to put it in the hands of God. If it was meant to be, it would be. If not... she would just have to figure out something else.

She was lost in such thoughts when there came a knock at the door. She jumped, gasping softly and nearly poking herself with the needle in her hand.

"I will answer," Lucy said, abandoning a sock which Sophia had given her to mend. It was one of her own old socks so that her younger sister could practice. And Sophia could see that while Lucy worked hard to learn what Sophia and their mother taught her about sewing, she would much rather be off doing things that all normal twelve-year-old girls from families who did not have such financial troubles were doing. As she should, Sophia thought with a heavy heart.

"Sister," Lucy said, rushing back into the room, breathless. "It is a letter for you."

Sophia's heart stopped, and she took the letter with a trembling hand. Within the envelope, she found a note with a simple message.

Dear Miss Hartley,

We have found a potential governess position suitable for you. Please return to our office at your earliest convenience.

Sincerely,
Tomalin Abernathy

Sophia stared at the letter with wide eyes. Her excitement mounted, and she ran from the room into the kitchen, where her mother was surveying the near empty cabinets. She thrust the letter into her mother's hands, thrilled to see a small smile on her mother's face.

"This is wonderful, darling," she said. "When will you be going to the newspaper office?"

Sophia folded up the letter, putting it in the pocket of her worn gray dress.

"I shall go right away," she said.

With a quick kiss to the cheeks of both her mother and sister, Sophia flew to the small room she shared with Lucy, rummaging through her dresser and her handful of dresses. She dug until she reached the bottom, retrieving the best dress she had; a gift from her father for her birthday, shortly before he fell ill. It was a lavender dress, which was her favorite color. Its satin fabric felt cool and slick beneath her fingers. It was the last nice thing her father had ever bought for her.

In that moment, she felt as though she were receiving the gift from him twice. She had not worn the dress since they had gone to Gunter's for shaved ices for her birthday. It was still fresh looking, with no stains or worn spots. And she had never needed such a pretty, flawless looking dress as much as she did right then.

She hurriedly dressed, refreshed the bun in her hair and pulled on some black boots. Her mother had made her some lavender gloves for Christmastide the previous year that were only a shade darker than her dress. She donned those, then rushed out of the house to hail a hired hack. She could have walked, as she had the previous time. But she did not want to risk getting her new, crisp dress dirty.

A hack stopped a moment later, and she shoved silver coins into the driver's hands, climbing aboard. She kept her expression pleasant, but her nerves were on fire. She was thrilled that after she was told not to expect to be contacted for the position of a governess, they had done just that, and in just a couple of days. However, she was also terrified. There was still a chance that they would not have a guaranteed position for her. They still needed to vet her for any positions they found for her, as did the potential employers themselves. She could still find herself without employment, even at that stage. And if that happened, she would remain helpless to be an asset to her family's financial situation.

As the hack made its way through the crowded streets of London, her mind continued to race. Surely, there was a chance she would fail to get this position. But she was allowing herself to dismiss the possibility that she might not fail, also.

She was also forgetting that even if she missed the chance for this job, there would surely be offers for others, especially if she showed the proper enthusiasm about being called to discuss jobs. The important thing right then was for her to remember that securing work was the key to ensuring that her sister and mother had a better life. That was all that truly mattered to Sophia.

But what if there are not other offers? She thought, chewing her lip. What if Mrs. Abernathy tosses my information in the bin if I am unable to secure this job without experience or references?

She exhaled deeply, using all her mental force to push such thoughts aside. They would do nothing but make her even more nervous than she already was. And she could not allow Mrs. Abernathy to see that she was rattled and feeling so unsure of herself. She was out to prove that she was confident in her skills, not the contrary.

When the hack reached the office, Sophia had most of her wits about her. Seeing the place again caused another surge of nervousness, but she quelled it by reminding herself that there was too much at stake for her to fumble it with her fear. She walked into the agency with her head held high, smiling at Mrs. Abernathy, despite the fact that the woman's steely, frigid gaze made her want to turn and run.

"Come," the firm woman said, motioning to Sophia. "I would speak with you more in depth, about your background, your constitution and the like."

Sophia's heart fluttered, but she maintained her calm façade.

"Yes, Mrs. Abernathy," she said, joining the lanky, bitter woman at a table in the lobby.

The woman stacked some papers in front of her, pulling her spectacles down to the tip of her sharp nose as she read. Then, she peered at Sophia over the top of the rims, causing Sophia to shiver. The woman truly looked as though she could be a witch from a storybook. She acted like it, too.

"It seems that the position available to you is a governess position at Rollins Manor," she said. "Your employers would be the dowager viscountess, Lady Augusta Rollins, and the current reigning viscount, Lord Julian Rollins."

Sophia nodded. Her anticipation was making it difficult for her to focus on what the woman was saying. She forced herself to concentrate, committing every word, that she possibly could, to memory.

"Very well," she said. "What else must I know for this position?"

Mrs. Abernathy smirked at her, shaking her head.

"First, I must ask you a few questions," she said.

Sophia swallowed again, but she kept her smile as she nodded once more.

"Very well," she repeated.

The hard woman raised an eyebrow as she searched for another sheet of paper. She raised it to just below eye level so that she could glance over it at Sophia.

"Have you ever been arrested?" she asked.

Sophia had to choke down her indignation. It would not do to snap at the one person who could successfully get her hired for work she desperately needed.

"No, I have not," she said, trying to sound as sweet as she could, as opposed to bitter.

Mrs. Abernathy looked her over, nodding.

"I should think not," she said. "I suppose you also have not committed any crimes that have not been discovered by the authorities."

Sophia shook her head. She was not accustomed to being asked such questions. She supposed she understood the reason for it. But it was still strange to her that she was having to answer things that, to her, seemed perfectly obvious, and a little offensive.

"I have never done anything illegal or immoral," she said.

The woman nodded, sniffing. Sophia expected her to say something else snappy. But instead, she just shrugged.

"Very well," she said. "I can believe that you are not much of a troublemaker. And I have already spoken with the local authorities, and they have never so much as heard of you, which tells me that you are at least telling the truth about never being arrested. You have one offer for a job right now. And since you have passed the interview here, you will move on to being interviewed by the employer himself."

Sophia's head was spinning so fast that it took her a minute to understand what the woman had just said.

"A job offer?" she echoed.

Mrs. Abernathy snickered and nodded.

"You will be responsible for the education of two children, ages seven and nine. One boy, one girl, and son and daughter to the Viscount Rollins."

Sophia did her best to appear as though she was hanging onto every word the woman spoke. But she was so excited and relieved that it was all she could do to catch the important parts of what the woman was saying. After all her worry and stress, there was a job for her. It didn't matter who her employer would be, or how many children they had. She would just have to be sure to be prepared for the direct interview with the employer. She could not be as unsure of herself then as she had been with Mrs. Abernathy.

"Miss Hartley?" the woman said sharply, drawing her attention back to the present moment. "I want to be sure that you understand that you have secured this position, despite your lack of references. This is very important, and I must ensure that you know what that means."

Sophia blinked. She thought she would need to pass another interview. What employer would hire her without experience, at least without meeting her?

"Oh?" she asked, trying to swallow her apprehension.

Mrs. Abernathy smirked and nodded.

"Be prepared to depart in two days," she said. "Lord and the dowager Lady Rollins will send a carriage to collect you. They are a wealthy noble family, and they have used our help many times."

Sophia was nodding, but the last thing the woman said stuck with her. If the family had used their help many times, what did that mean?

She shook her head, smiling as she rose from her seat. She did not care what had happened to the other employees of the Rollins family. If she had secured the position, she would do everything in her power to retain it. And how bad could it be if the family had two young children?

"Thank you so very much, Mrs. Abernathy," she said, reaching out to shake the woman's hand. The woman looked at her as though her fingers were snakes, so Sophia withdrew slowly. Mrs. Abernathy looked back at her, her smirk growing.

"You should also know that the reason you secured the position so quickly, despite you lacking everything required to get a job through us, is that no one ever wants to work with Lord Rollins for very long."

Sophia was too thrilled to have the job to be overly concerned right in that moment with why no one wanted to remain employed with Lord Rollins. However, something told her that she should at least inquire about the subject, since Mrs. Abernathy was making such a point to mention it.

"Is there a specific reason why?" she asked, suddenly hoping that Mrs. Abernathy was merely trying to spook her.

The woman nodded, smirking at Sophia once more.

"We connect many noble families with employees all throughout London," she said. "However, Lord Rollins has been known to frighten all our employees with his frosty demeanor. In fact, that is all which is known about him, according to most of the ladies we have sent to him. Many governesses have come and gone with him. I do hope that you will be different."

Sophia knew she should be concerned. If she was starting out her tenure as a governess with a difficult employer, one wrong move could render her unable to find work in London ever again. But how could this woman be so sure that the rumors she had heard were true? Perhaps, the other employees who had left the Rollins' household had found other jobs or had found themselves in legitimate trouble with their employer. It did not mean that she would have the same experience with Lord Rollins.

"Much obliged, nonetheless," she said, smiling brightly once more. She was determined not to let gossip trouble her, especially when her spirits were soaring. She was sure that Mrs. Abernathy was exaggerating, even if she truly believed the women who had spoken to her about the viscount. "I shall take my leave now. I hope you have a wonderful day."

Mrs. Abernathy looked both surprised and disgusted by Sophia's continued optimism. But Sophia remained undeterred. She waved a final goodbye to the woman, rushing out the door and into the warm spring sunshine.

Her mind raced as she hurried home. She was more excited than she had ever been. However, despite her efforts, she was also more than a little nervous after what Mrs. Abernathy had said. She refused to believe any gossip without proof, and the most important thing was that the job opportunity could be exactly what she needed to change her family's fortune and future. But even though she would not give in to speculation about unsubstantiated rumors, she could not stop thinking about what Mrs. Abernathy had said.

No, she chided herself firmly. You cannot say you do not believe gossip while believing gossip. She blushed, even though she was the only one who could hear her thoughts and scolding. It was true, and she knew it. She could not be so contradictory and expect to have any peace. She would either believe gossip spread by a very cold, callused woman, or she would believe none of it. And she chose the latter.

"Mother, Lucy," Sophia said, bursting through the door of the small apartment as her excitement won over the trepidation. "I have a job."

Chapter Four

Julian stared at the letter in his hand. It arrived just that morning from the newspaper office through which he had requested a governess. It was a wonder to him that they would still consider him as a viable employer, considering that he had been through five of their governesses in just over a year's time. He might be a wealthy viscount, but he was certain that even money and status would only go so far. Earning a reputation as an employer with a high turnover rate could not be good, even among the most esteemed individuals in ton. He did not care, however. It was not his fault that every one of his governesses found some reason to leave.

According to the letter, the most suitable candidate, one Miss Sophia Hartley, would be arriving the following day to begin her duties. He sighed, thinking about the most recent governess to leave his employ. Of all the ones who had terminated their own tenure with him, she had been the one with the most viable excuse. And yet part of him doubted that she had been truthful.

She had left after a dispute about the books she had borrowed from the library to tutor Henry and Elizabeth. They were romance books, which she had claimed she was using strictly for the purposes of expanding their vocabulary. But he had determined the books inappropriate for a seven- and nine-year-old. He had forbidden, rather firmly, her from using such books. She had hurried away from him crying. Then two days later, she resigned.

As he read the letter regarding Miss Hartley, he pinched the bridge of his nose. It seemed that she did not have any professional experience as a governess, and that was almost enough for him to toss out the letter and request a different candidate. But he thought again about the other governesses who had left. Perhaps, to prevent any future trouble with the office, he should be grateful they were willing to send anyone at all.

I do hope Miss Hartley can prove herself to be more resilient than the governesses before her, though, he thought. If only Eliza was still here...

With the arrangements already made for the new potential governess to arrive the next day, there was nothing more for him to do on the matter. Doing his best to avoid glancing at the portrait which hung on the wall opposite his desk, he set to work looking through the paperwork from his steward that detailed all the payments owed to his employees.

It was a simple enough task. But Julian kept thinking about the following day and the inconvenience of having to take part of his day to speak with what would likely be his new governess. He considered handing over the matter to his mother. But given her recent meddling with his perpetual widower's status, he did not think that was a good idea.

As the clock struck five o'clock, Julian closed his ledgers and went to his chambers. He summoned his valet, then waited with weighted dread for Alexander to come help him dress for his mother's accursed dinner party. He idly chose a black suit, of which he had many, as he saw little point in caving to the latest colorful clothing trends when he had no practical use for fashion. Mother will be thrilled, he thought humorlessly.

The guest list included his brother and sister-in-law, whom he loved dearly. But it also included Lady Irene and her parents, the earl and countess of Locshire. He would rather have his hand caught in a horse-drawn carriage door than to spend any part of an evening with the latter three guests. Especially when he knew perfectly well that the evening would be filled with drab polite conversation and matchmaking attempts so thinly veiled that they would vanish in drinking water.

When Alexander reached his chambers, he held out the suit, giving his valet a wordless order. Alexander took the suit, undressing his master with the same silence that Julian was offering. The expression on Alexander's face spoke of curiosity and intrigue, no doubt wondering what inspired Julian to attend a social event. But Julian would not indulge the man's unasked question. He wanted to be dressed and head downstairs as quickly as possible. The sooner he could begin the night, the sooner he could end it.

He reached the dining room doors just as the other guests did. His mother gave him the briefest of warning glances, no doubt upset at having to greet the guests alone. He blatantly ignored the ice in his mother's eyes, moving to embrace his brother with a small smile.

"George," he said, clapping his younger brother on the back. "It is good to see you."

George stepped back, casting an inconspicuous glance toward their mother.

"I think Mother will have words for you later," he said in a low voice, giving his older brother a sly wink. "You know how she hates to be tardy at social events."

Julian snorted softly, moving toward Susan.

"And I shall have none for her," he said. "I do not share her love of social events." And one so informal, and hosted in my own home, is no exception.

After a quick kiss to Susan's cheek, Julian greeted the rest of the guests as they filed into the dining room. He muttered excuses about working late to explain him being late to greet them. Lord and Lady Locshire smiled politely and graciously. Lady Irene, however, batted her eyes so rapidly that she looked like a grounded butterfly trying to take wing. Still, Julian gave her no attention beyond the socially expected greeting which he had given to her parents, as well.

Once inside the grand dining room, the guests all took their places around the elegantly set mahogany table. He was pleased to find that his mother had not taken the liberty of seating Lady Irene beside him. However, he was hardly surprised when he looked up to realize that she was seated directly across from him. He instantly regretted taking his eyes off his place setting. Lady Irene met his gaze with a flirty one of her own, smiling coyly at him.

"This is such a lovely dining room, Lord Rollins," she said. "You must have amassed great wealth to have such fine décor."

Julian shrugged. He did not feel that he should have to tell the young lady that the dining room décor had been handled by his parents, only maintained rather than updated since shortly after his own birth. He did not think that it was a direct play to learn just how much wealth Julian had. However, he also knew that it would tell the woman precisely that, even if it was just how it sounded: a poor attempt at sounding affluent and wise in the ways of money and the world.

"Indeed," he said flatly, only his thoughts belying his sarcasm.

The young lady batted her eyelashes at him, fanning her face delicately with a small fan as they awaited the first course of the meal.

"Your suit looks very dashing on you," she said. "It is of very high quality, and it looks as though it was tailored just for you."

At this, she giggled, and Julian understood that she must have been trying to tell a joke. He caught the joke, sure enough. But he had no interest in laughing at a flattering remark that turned into such a terrible joke.

"It was, in fact," he said.

As confusion and disappointment flashed in Lady Irene's eyes, Julian had to stifle a bitter scoff. She was not very intelligent, and she was already mentioning his family fortune, no matter in what context. Two more reasons to reject Lady Irene, and the entire prospect of remarriage, he thought dryly.

But Lady Irene was not to be so easily deterred. She gave him a shy smile and looked into his eyes.

"I do prattle on like a silly girl, do I not?" she asked. "Tell me about your interests."

Julian blinked, keeping his stoic mask fixed and unyielding. As their respective parents were watching the two of them closely, Julian could not simply dismiss her question. Nor could he be too callused with his response. Yet nor could he abide engaging in a full conversation with her about any topics. Any such attempt would be viewed by her as an interest in courtship. His entire body tensed with the strain, but he refused to allow his expression to change.

"I enjoy books," he said. "And horseback riding." *Two things which I am sure are of little interest to a refined woman such as yourself,* he thought with an inward grimace.

The faltering expression on the young lady's face confirmed

what he thought. But she was still on a mission to earn his attention.

"I imagine you look most handsome sitting atop a noble steer," she said. Her voice was dreamy and just nauseating enough to keep Julian from laughing at her clumsy wording.

"I believe the word is steed," he said. It was cruel to correct and embarrass her in front of guests. But she was being rude by insisting to speak to someone during a meal who had no interest in conversing. And in his own home, no less. It was in poor taste, and that would never be of any interest to Julian.

George, ever perceptive, gave Julian an understanding nod. The young lady did not see it, but Julian was grateful when his brother spoke.

"This spring has certainly been rather lovely, has it not?" he asked.

Julian nodded, smirking at his brother. A discussion about weather, Brother? He wondered silently. George shrugged, smiling back at his older brother.

Lady Irene was as clueless as ever. She giggled, batting her eyelashes at Julian once more.

"Lovely, indeed," she said. "I believe it is perfect weather to attend small picnics along the Thames and walks during Promenade Hour."

Julian glanced at George, who looked at him sheepishly. George's attempt to divert the conversation to something more casual failed. Julian did not blame his brother, however. Lady Irene was clearly trying to force Julian's hand into inviting her to a social outing.

Little did she know that he was as determined to ignore such efforts as she was to succeed with them. She wanted to put him in a position where his mother and her parents would expect him to arrange an outing for them. But all he wanted was to retreat back to his study, back to the memory of his beloved late wife and far away from her and from the glances that his mother and her parents kept giving the two of them. He did not wish to think any longer about what was expected of him. He wanted to be alone with his thoughts, away from such pressures.

When dinner finally ended, Julian was too happy to retire to the billiard room. However, when the gentlemen excused themselves from the table, Julian remembered that that included Lord Locshire, as well as his younger brother. George set up a round of billiards, while Julian poured the three men snifters of brandy. He put on his best host smile as he passed around the glasses, eager to begin the game.

"I suppose it would be very ungentlemanly to place a wager on this game," the earl of Locshire said with a bellowing laugh, clearly pleased with his own stale joke.

Julian and George laughed, and George took over the conversation.

"I wager that you would lose, Lord Locshire," he said, grinning. "My brother and I cannot be beaten when it comes to billiards."

The earl chuckled again, but the expression on his face said that he believed the younger Rollins son.

"I do not doubt that for a moment," he said. "Besides, the joy of seeing my darling Irene thriving within society since coming out are more than enough excitement for me right now. Her future happiness is of the utmost importance to me, and I know that she will find such happiness when she finds the right marriage match for her and begins having a family of her own. There is nothing more fulfilling in life, after all."

Julian glanced at George, who blanched just as Julian himself did. The unspoken message was clear, but Julian was no more willing to take the earl's hint than he had been to take the hints of his daughter. He politely nodded, forcing his smile to remain steadfast.

"Indeed," he said calmly. "Whose turn is it again?"

George grinned once more, stepping forward.

"I believe it is mine," he said. "Do not fret, Brother. I will leave enough desire in the earl so that you may play against him, as well."

Despite the company and aid of his younger brother in keeping the earl occupied until the evening finally ended, Julian was relieved to bid his guests farewell at the conclusion of the night. He retired to his chambers no sooner than the front door of the mansion had closed behind George. The instant quiet comfort of solitude instantly relaxed Julian. But it also brought back the vulnerability of loneliness as he thought, as ever, about Eliza.

Without his late wife, the future was completely uncertain. And everyone, including an earl who was barely an acquaintance, seemed to have opinions and plans for what Julian should do. Julian's life was beginning to feel less like his own and more like it belonged to perfect strangers. Or, at the very least, his own mother. How I wish that Eliza could show me what I must do... if only one last time.

Chapter Five

"Sister, please, do not go," Lucy said, sobbing as she threw her arms around her older sister.

Sophia embraced her sister tightly, holding onto her for as long as she could before she released her and stepped back.

"Darling girl, I must," she said, trying to sound braver than she felt. It had occurred to her, as she checked to ensure she had all her things packed, that she might be saying goodbye to her mother and sister for a very long time, or perhaps even indefinitely.

She did not dare voice the thought, however. Although she suspected that her mother knew the same fact, she also believed that her mother held onto the hope that Sophia would be able to visit often. Sophia herself wanted to believe that. But if any of what she had heard about her potential employer was true, she could not count on such a luxury.

Caroline pulled her hysterical younger daughter to her side, hugging Sophia fiercely with the other hand.

"I am so proud of you, sweetheart," she said, kissing Sophia's cheek as tears rolled down her own. "It pains me that you must do this. But I understand it is for the best, and I wish you all the luck, and send you off with all my love."

At their mother's words, Lucy burst into tears again. Sophia embraced the two people she loved most in the entire world, fighting back her own tears. She had to be brave and show nothing but excitement, even though she was filled with sorrow and apprehension.

"I promise to write to you as often as I possibly can," she said, smiling a little too brightly. "And I promise to send you money the instant I receive my first pay, and from every payment I receive after that. I will see to it that the two of you never go hungry again."

Lucy was still crying with her face against their mother's bosom. But after a long silence, she nodded to show that she understood her sister.

Caroline kissed her younger daughter's head, then gently pushed Sophia toward the drive, up which a carriage was slowly rolling.

"Go, my sweet Sophia," she said. "We shall await word from you."

Sophia nodded, biting her cheek to choke back a sob.

"I love you both so very much," she said.

Lucy muffled her sobs in her mother's embrace, but Sophia heard her words clearly.

"I love you more, dear sister," she said.

Their mother wiped away her tears and nodded.

"You are half my heart, darling," she said.

With that, Sophia turned her back to the only people who could ever mean the world to her. She waited for the carriage, which was a brilliant, freshly shined white trimmed with dark brown and pulled by two white horses. As it rolled to a stop, a footman leapt down and fetched her single trunk. He loaded it on the back of the carriage, then helped her inside the coach. She waved goodbye to her mother and sister as the carriage pulled away from her home, holding back her tears until they were well out of sight.

As the carriage rolled along the narrow country roads leading from London to the smaller villages to the north, Sophia admired the scenery. It changed from tall buildings and clouds billowing from smokestacks to brilliant green grass and tall trees within a few moments of crossing the northeastern edge of London proper. The houses turned into large mansions and estates, and the potted plants became patches of yellow, orange, pink, red and white wildflowers. It was a peaceful journey, and Sophia enjoyed looking at the wonders of nature all around her, as she had once loved to do in her spare time during walks around the grounds at their old townhouse.

She missed those nature walks since having to spend all her time helping with the sewing work. And it was nice to get a little taste of nature, even though the carriage moved a bit faster than she did during her walks. Nevertheless, the invigorating breeze bolstered her spirits for the challenges that awaited her. Yet, it did not entirely dispel the trepidation that lingered within her. She kept thinking of what Mrs. Abernathy had said to her about the viscount.

She did not know what she should expect upon her arrival. And as hard as she tried, it was difficult not to imagine Lord Rollins being an ogre of a man. As much as she needed employment, she did not know if she could handle someone with such a disposition.

You are being ridiculous, she thought, admonishing herself. She was once again allowing her thoughts to be controlled by gossip that she had no way of confirming for herself. At least, not until she arrived at Rollins Manor. It was possible that the viscount was a perfectly lovely, if eccentric, gentleman who simply found himself at odds with some of his previous staff members. But although she tempered her judgment of the viscount, she could not tame her nervousness. What if he hired her and gave her hope of being able to save her family, just to dismiss her in a few weeks?

She shook her head just as the carriage rolled up the long drive to Rollins Manor about an hour later. The vast mansion was formidable, compared to the small apartment she had shared with her mother and sister. The cream-colored walls were immaculate and warm. But she could not see anything through any of the windows, despite the curtains on the first floor being pulled aside. The entire inside of the mansion appeared dark, and she shivered. Surely, the interior was not as cold as it appeared from the outside.

A short, thin man dressed in a butler's uniform held open the door for her when she and the footman, who unloaded her trunk, entered the manor.

"Miss Hartley, I presume?" he asked. He was perfectly polite, but his tone was guarded beneath its professionalism.

Sophia nodded, curtseying.

"I am," she said.

He gave her an uncertain but kind smile.

"I am Wyatt," he said, gesturing to a tall, round woman behind him. "And this is Mrs. Barnes. She will be introducing you to the staff members and showing you to your quarters. I shall go inform the lord and lady of the house of your arrival. It is best for you to keep on your best behaviour."

Sophia nodded, swallowing. There was no ominous tone in Wyatt's voice. But he sounded most sincere, and even a little concerned.

Mrs. Barnes snorted, regaining Sophia's attention.

"Best behaviour, indeed," she said, her words not nearly as polite or professional as those of Wyatt. Her gaze of appraisal made Sophia feel far from confident in herself. But Sophia was determined to make a good impression.

"It is a pleasure to meet you," she said. "I am delighted for the opportunity to be in Lord Rollins' employ."

Mrs. Barnes snickered again, looking Sophia over once more.

"Indeed," she repeated. "You will find that the only thing anyone cares about here is work getting done. And there is to be no effort made to make yourself a favourite with Lord and Lady Rollins. It is a useless endeavour and highly frowned upon, especially with the two of them. Just do your job and do not make trouble." Mrs. Barnes narrowed her eyes and raised her eyebrows. "Of any sort."

Sophia nodded. She did not wish to make any trouble. She did not know if it was wise to say as much, or to tell the formidable housekeeper why. But she decided that, if she were to be under scrutiny, particularly from multiple people in the household, honesty would likely be her dearest friend.

"I assure you that I will not make any trouble," she said, letting her sincerity shine through her smile. "My family and I need this income too badly. And I feel fortunate enough as it is to have found employment so soon after applying."

At this, the housekeeper's expression softened, but only in the slightest. Sophia could see through the housekeeper's expression a reluctant desire to trust her, as well as something that resembled the way the butler had looked at her. But she tried to push the unease aside as she waited for Mrs. Barnes to begin the tour.

"Very well," the stout woman said, turning on her heel and marching in the other direction. "Follow me, Miss Hartley."

Sophia complied. As they wove through the mansion, Sophia

took in the wood floors and the thick, soft blue and green rugs that covered them. Sophia glimpsed the music room, the library, the first-floor parlor, one of two sitting rooms on the first floor and the cellar, which was filled wall-to-wall with wine racks.

"We shall start by introducing you to the cook," she said, leading Sophia to the kitchens. "It will be your responsibility to see to it that the children get lunch, whether by your hand or that of the nursemaid."

Sophia nodded, putting her warm smile back into place.

"I will remember that," she said.

The housekeeper sniffed, but she said nothing more as she continued leading the way. Sophia tried to memorize each room as she passed it, but she knew that she would need to locate each one herself to accurately find them on her own.

When they reached the kitchens, there were two women standing there. Sophia could not help noticing the tense silence as the three older employees shared a look, then glanced at her. She swallowed, trying to ignore the return of the same apprehension she had experienced when she was speaking with Mrs. Abernathy.

"Rebecca, Mrs. Brewer," Mrs. Barnes said. "This is the new governess, Sophie Harley."

Sophia bit her lip, wondering if she should correct the abrupt woman.

"Forgive me," she said, almost too softly to be audible. "But it's Sophia Hartley."

The cook, a sturdy, olive-skinned woman, snorted and shook her head.

"No matter," she said. "You will not be here long enough for anyone to learn your name."

The red-headed woman whom Mrs. Barnes had called Rebecca stepped forward, giving Sophia a tentative smile.

"It is a pleasure to meet you, Sophia," she said. "I do hope that you settle in nicely here."

Mrs. Barnes and Mrs. Brewer exchanged looks once again. Then, Mrs. Barnes clapped her hands together, giving Sophia a curt nod.

"Very well then, Sophia," she said, emphasizing the

correction to Sophia's name. "Let us continue with the tour. You will want to be settled in and rested before tomorrow morning."

Sophia nodded, smiling primarily at Rebecca who, so far, was the only person who had been kind to her.

"It was lovely to meet the two of you," she said.

The cook's expression softened, and she nodded.

"Likewise," she said. "Come talk to me or Rebecca for the children's lunches."

Sophia nodded, relaxing, if only marginally.

"Thank you very much," she said.

Rebecca and Mrs. Brewer nodded, and Mrs. Barnes abruptly exited the kitchens. They concluded the tour on the second floor which, apart from another sitting room and parlor and a washroom, was comprised of the chambers for the lord and lady of the house and guest rooms. Mrs. Barnes, pointed to the short staircase at the end of the hallway opposite Lord Rollins' chambers.

"Your room will be up on the third floor," she said. "Come. I shall take you to it, and then leave you to get settled."

Sophia nodded, offering a weak smile. The anxiety of the day was catching up to her, and she realized she was ready for a moment of solitude.

As they reached the third floor landing, they passed by three maids who had been whispering amongst themselves. They shared a look as Sophia approached, then they regarded Sophia with wide eyes. She nodded as Mrs. Barnes ushered her to her room, which was smaller than the second-floor washroom had been. Once she was inside, the housekeeper crossed the room back to the doorway in three steps, clasping her hands together in front of her.

"Breakfast will be served at seven sharp," she said. "You will be expected to eat and be prepared to begin your duties at seven thirty. Do not be late."

Sophia nodded once more, and the housekeeper closed the door firmly behind her. Alone at last, Sophia glanced down at the hard straw bed. The gray of the sheets matched the gray, modest uniform that sat atop it, reminding Sophia of her new status. As a merchant's daughter, she was accustomed to not having a noble title. She was not, however, accustomed to working for nobility.

How I wish Lucy were here, she thought wistfully as a longing for her home overwhelmed her. She knew that her job as governess would ease the financial burden off her mother and sister, and that was more important than anything to Sophia. But she could not deny that she already missed her family and their small, worn home. Nor could she ignore the pressure she felt regarding her new duties. And with the servants all seeming either cold or eager to avoid her, she could not help wondering if there was some truth to what Mrs. Abernathy had told her.

With a deep breath, Sophia began to unpack her things. She could not allow the future, as uncertain as it might be, to overwhelm her, especially before she had even begun her job. She needed to remain optimistic and focused if she were to be able to save her family. Rebecca seemed nice enough. And it did not truly matter if she made any friends. All that mattered was that her job performance was satisfactory so that she could keep her position.

When her hand settled on a cold chain, Sophia gasped softly. She pulled the metal out of the bottom of one of her trunks, discovering a small, worn locket. She opened it, finding a tiny portrait of her father inside. There was a smile on his face, and it brought tears to her eyes. She held the necklace tightly to her chest, allowing her father's memory to grant her strength.

Things might not be easy for her in the beginning of her new journey. But if there was anything she had learned from her father, it was that love and sacrifices were necessary to protect and care for those she loved. She would be as prepared as she could possibly be to meet the Rollins family and to begin her duties the following day. She had no choice but to succeed if she wanted to make sure that her mother and sister had a better life.

Chapter Six

Two days after the arrival of the letter announcing the arrival of the new governess, Julian summoned Alexander, who set about helping him dress in his usual contemplative silence. Julian appreciated that he and Alexander had such a relationship that the valet did not feel the need to engage him in needless conversation. Even before Eliza died, Alexander had been a man of few words. While Julian did not doubt the valet's loyalty or feelings regarding his employer, Julian was grateful to have one less person with whom to converse, when he preferred to exist in his memories more often than not.

When he was ready, he pulled himself down the stairs to join his mother in the grand dining hall for breakfast. He gave the dowager a curt nod before taking his place at the long dining table. Even as he filled his plate with porridge and fruit, he could feel his mother's gaze on him, her eagerness to converse with him radiating off her like chill off a mountain of snow.

He had barely taken his first bite of his meal before Augusta spoke.

"Dinner was just lovely last night, was it not?" she said.

Julian shuddered at the gushing in her tone, keeping his focus on his plate.

"Indeed," he said, tempering his sarcasm with bland disinterest.

His mother did not seem to notice. She gave him a smile, which he could see from the corner of his eye, helping herself to a bite of her own meal before speaking again.

"And Lady Irene," she said with a breathy sigh. "She is even lovelier and more refined than I first believed."

Julian kept his expression neutral, even as his blood began to simmer. He had found Lady Irene to be nothing but an opportunistic, shallow girl with nothing more intriguing to say than about her alleged interest in his life. He could not believe that someone, as regal as his mother had been before his father's death, could suffer such company. But then, he supposed that one could suffer a great deal if one were obsessed on making one's family look good.

"Would you pass the grapes, Mother?" he asked. He was hardly in the mood to discuss the dinner, or Lady Irene, or anything, for that matter. He hoped to avoid an argument with his mother by simply dismissing the subject. But the dowager would not be deterred. She motioned for a maid to fetch the bowl of grapes in front of her seat. As the maid carried them to Julian, she spoke yet again.

"Darling, I truly do think that Lady Irene would make a very lovely match for you," she said.

Julian clenched his jaw, fighting with all his willpower to swallow his irritation.

"I am certain that you do," he muttered, keeping his voice as quiet as he could manage.

"What was that, Julian?" his mother asked. He did not think she had heard him, but he was sure she could guess that he had said something rather biting.

"It is a lovely day for a trip into town for a little shopping, wouldn't you say, Mother?" he asked, once more trying to divert the subject.

The dowager looked at him, clearly understanding what it was that he was trying to do. But still she pressed on, reminding Julian of how lovely she thought Lady Irene had been in her gown, the color of which Julian had already forgotten. His agitation rose, and he tried his best to simply focus on his food. He truly did not wish for an argument with his mother. However, it did not matter to him how much she pressed and kept returning to the subject. He had no intention whatsoever of entertaining her notions of marriage, or of Lady Irene. And he certainly did not intend to listen to his mother prattle on about any of it.

He ate slowly and deliberately as his appetite had waned the instant his mother had mentioned Lady Irene. But it was the easiest way he could tune out his mother's droning about the young lady. He knew that his mother would know he was not listening. He was also aware that she would likely keep bringing it up, determined to make him cave on the matter. But for the time being, the best he could do was to allow her to speak her mind and hope that would silence her for a while.

Julian was so lost in his efforts to ignore his mother that he did not notice the silence that fell between them. Not until his mother broke the quiet once more.

"I suppose you are aware that the new governess arrived yesterday," she said, clearly annoyed with Julian.

Julian shook his head. How could I be aware of that, when all you have done is prattle on about Lady Irene? He thought dryly.

"I was not," he said. "Although I was told we should expect her yesterday, as per the letter I received."

The dowager, seeming pleased to have finally gotten a response from him, nodded curtly.

"She arrived on time, just as expected," she said. "That speaks a little to her character."

Julian nodded. That conversation was not much more appealing to him than that about Lady Irene. But at least, it had far less mention of marriage.

"Wonderful," he said blandly. "She can begin her duties this morning."

His mother cleared her throat, forcing Julian to look at her. She was practically glaring at him, which made him bristle.

"I plan to interview the young woman myself before introducing her to the children," she said.

The annoyance, which had just begun to die, rose within Julian anew, threatening to drown him in its sudden tidal wave. He set down his knife and fork with a loud clang against the plate, returning his mother's narrow-eyed gaze.

"I wish to be present for the interview, as well," he said. That was not the truth. He wanted nothing less, in fact. But his mother was becoming too controlling, and he was getting tired of it. "As their father, it is my duty to ensure that the governess is well suited for this position and that she will make a good addition to our staff and our household. As Henry's and Elizabeth's father, it is my duty to ensure that the new governess is suitable for the position, and a good fit for our family, as well."

The dowager looked at her son with a mixture of awe and skepticism.

"It is wonderful that you are taking such an interest in what happens with them," she said in a tone that Julian could not quite read. "If you would like to interview the governess with me, you are welcome to do so. But I would like to remind you that I am your mother, and you will mind your tone with me and cease these outbursts."

Julian scoffed at his mother. The disrespect he was incurring over her ideas of remarriage and a mother figure for the children would never be addressed. And his mother forgot that he, as lord of the house, was to have his every order obeyed and not to be contradicted or overruled, especially by a woman.

"I shall meet you in the east drawing room in one hour," he said, cooling his tone to near freezing.

Augusta blinked, clearly surprised that Julian had not groveled as he did when he was a child after a scolding. But after a moment, she rose and left the room. Julian followed suit, locking himself in his chambers for the next hour. He saw no need to change out of the dark brown suit in which Alexander had helped him dress. He was only meeting a governess. Why would he ever wish to impress an employee?

Despite spending the time staring blankly out his chamber window, an hour passed more rapidly than Julian expected. The grandfather clock struck, startling him from thoughts about Eliza. He grimaced. He had told his mother that he wanted to see for himself if the governess was suitable for his children, and it was not entirely a lie. However, he also knew he would not have said it if his mother had not been so overbearing. The last thing he wanted to do right then was to be forced to speak with an employee, no matter how new she was.

Julian dragged himself down the stairs and into the drawing room. His mother was already waiting, sipping a cup of tea. He gave her a curt nod, walking over to the fireplace and fixing his gaze firmly on the door. His mother did not seem to have any conversation for him, and that suited him perfectly. He guessed that she did not wish for the new governess to hear any sharp words between them. And Julian did not wish to speak any words to her at all.

The twenty minutes that passed while they waited for the entrance of the governess were filled with icy silence. He pushed aside his feelings about his recent interactions with his mother and thought about any questions he might have for the governess. But even then, all he could think about was Eliza, and how none of that would be necessary if she were alive. He wished the woman would hurry. He wanted to set her on the task of educating the children and then pretending she did not exist, just as he did with the other servants.

When Mrs. Barnes entered the room, however, Julian frowned. She was accompanied only by one woman. A very young woman, to be precise, not more than twenty years old. She was wearing a governess's uniform, but she was impossibly beautiful, and the smile on her face was warm, if a bit nervous. Her blue eyes were just as warm as the expression on her face, and pink cheeks drew his attention to freckles that lightly dusted her nose.

"This is Sophia Hartley," Mrs. Barnes said, curtseying to Julian and his mother. "Miss Hartley, this is Lord and Lady Rollins."

The dowager rose and dipped her head. Julian, realizing that he was still staring, fixed his face into a mask of disinterest and impartiality. Still, he waited for his mother to speak, trying to gather himself after the shock of the governess's youthful looks.

"Thank you for coming on such short notice, Miss Hartley," the dowager said. Her voice had a cold, professional edge and Julian thought he saw the governess flinch. But she recovered so quickly that Julian thought he must have been mistaken.

"I thank you for trusting me with this position," she said. Her voice was melodic and soft, and warmer than her eyes. Julian bit his cheek to keep the surprise from registering on his face.

Augusta Rollins smiled, studying the young governess.

"You are considerably younger than the other women who have worked for us before," she said. "How much experience do you have working with children?"

The young woman blushed, glancing away. When she looked up again, she caught Julian's eyes for a brief moment. If his heart had not been frozen, it would have stopped. She truly was very lovely, and not just compared to the other governesses before her. He had to force himself to look at his mother. What was he thinking?

"I have helped my mother with my twelve-year-old sister's education since our father died," she said. "Unfortunately, I do not have any professional experience as a governess. But I am an avid reader, and education is my passion."

In Julian's mind, his mouth fell open and he gaped at the young woman with wide eyes. He was as surprised by her quiet strength, and he believed her when she said she enjoyed reading. There was something in her eyes, a certain intelligence, that women of the ton did not have. However, outwardly, he merely stared at her, waiting for his mother's response and forcing himself to have no other reaction, even though she caught him completely off guard.

"Well, we would prefer that our governess have some real experience with children," the dowager said. "However, we are in desperate need of someone immediately. And I suppose a twelve-year-old is better than no child at all to teach you something about how to educate children."

Julian cleared his throat, stepping forward.

"Tell me," he said. "What are some things in which you have tutored your sister? Which books have you read, and which subjects has she studied?"

The young woman gave him a polite smile. Her cheeks grew pinker, but her eyes did not waver.

"We have read Mary Shelley's Frankenstein," she said. "We have also read all of Shakespeare's works, and we even performed some of them for our parents, before my father died. We had to adapt the plays, but we thoroughly enjoyed it. Besides that, we have read nature books and learned about all the animals which are native to England, and we worked hard on arithmetic. Lucy was not good at it when she was younger, but now, she can solve any problem you put in front of her."

Julian listened, trying to focus on her words and not the sweet music of her tone. She spoke with confidence, despite being apparently nervous, and there was not a hint of deception in her face.

"This is all wonderful to hear," he said. "However, you cannot expect us to just take your word for it. How do we know that you are not just making all this up to gain the position, only to be a complete failure at tutoring?"

The young woman did not miss a beat. She maintained her smile, holding up her head high.

"That is a fair question," she said. "I can only assure you that I can prove myself within a week. If you feel that I am a failure, you may fire me and seek someone with experience. But I believe that I can prove myself to Lady Rollins and you."

Julian glanced at his mother, even though he had already made up his mind. Her poise and grace, even under the pressure he was putting on her, were as impressive as they were unsettling. And yet it made him certain that she was speaking the truth about her abilities. Besides, as she had pointed out, if she were incapable, he could do as she had mentioned and find someone else. Even though he already knew he did not want to do that.

Swallowing an odd flutter in his chest, Julian cleared his throat once more.

"Welcome to Rollins Manor, Miss Hartley," he said. "You will be expected to be ready to begin lessons before eight each morning. Rebecca will tell you where the children and the last governess left off before she left us. I, however, must go, as I have pressing business matters to which I must attend."

With that, he bowed and hurried from the room, avoiding his mother's curious glare. He went directly to his study, where he leaned against the closed door. His heart was racing, which disturbed him greatly. He did not understand his reaction to the new governess. Not only was she beautiful, but she was also easily one of the most intriguing people he had ever met.

All the more reason to avoid her, he thought, pouring himself a drink and walking to the study window. He had never made any efforts to get to know any of the other staff members. And there was no reason why he should start with Miss Hartley. All he needed to do was stay away from her, as he had initially planned, unless it was absolutely pertinent that he speak with her. Then, he would not end up distracted from his duties or betray the memory of his beloved Eliza.

Chapter Seven

Sophia watched as the Viscount Rollins rushed out of the room. He had brushed by her on his way and, although he had not been looking at her when he did so, she had smelled his cologne. It was not enough that she had memorized every speckle in his bright green eyes, but now she knew that he smelled like a forest sprinkled with morning dew. She had avoided looking directly at him as he exited. But now that he was gone, she stared dumbly out the door as though she might make him reappear. Part of her dreaded that thought. But part of her did not.

He had been quite intense as he delivered his part of the interview. His eyes bore into her in a way that none ever had, and he had not minced his words when questioning her or voicing his expectations. He was, in a word, as cold as Mrs. Abernathy had told her he was rumored to be. And yet she was only a little intimidated by him. She was also strangely intrigued by her new employer. It was clear that he was very strict and that he did not tolerate any foolishness. But it was just as apparent how handsome he was. That alone made her head spin, knowing that she was not supposed to even entertain such thoughts.

She took a deep breath to try to redirect her focus. It would never do to think of the man who had hired her as anything other than an employer. Especially not a gentleman of noble status. She could not even believe that she would ever notice something as arbitrary as the looks of the person who would be paying her to do such an important job. Yet even as she tried to clear her thoughts and put her attention back on the rest of the interview, his strong jawline and chin would not leave her mind. What was wrong with her?

Willing her thoughts to shift, she turned her attention back to the dowager viscountess. Her cheeks burned as she locked eyes with Lady Rollins. The older woman raised an eyebrow and looked her over, causing Sophia to squirm internally. But outwardly, she held her shoulders back and kept her perfectly polite smile fixed on her face.

"Are you all right?" the dowager asked, studying her.

Sophia quickly composed herself, nodding fervently.

"Yes, I am perfectly well," she said, widening her smile.

The dowager nodded slowly, as though not quite believing Sophia. However, she did not ask Sophia any further questions. About her wellbeing, at least.

"I would like to know more about your lessons with your sister," she said. "Did you teach her anything about penmanship? As you well know, Henry and Elizabeth have not had many proper lessons in which they learned to write. And I need not tell you how important it is that everyone knows how to write. While I am sure that you did well enough tutoring a twelve-year-old, I doubt that she needed as much help as my grandchildren will."

Sophia offered another smile. The dowager was only partly correct. Sophia had helped Lucy with many of her assignments, even though their parents had hired tutors for them. Lucy always felt more comfortable completing assignments with Sophia, and she had helped her younger sister practice signing her name when she was ten. She told the dowager as much, and the older woman nodded. Her expression was largely unreadable, but her lips turned up into something resembling a smile.

"And were you good at arithmetic?" she asked. "That is one lesson that is extremely important to both Julian and me."

Sophia nodded. Lucy had been the stronger of the two of them at arithmetic as she grew older. But Sophia had no doubt that she could teach two children under the ages of ten enough arithmetic to hold her job.

"I am very good at arithmetic," she said. "That is my sister's strongest subject now, and we did all of our assignments together."

Lady Rollins nodded again. She paused for a moment, seemingly thinking over something. Sophia held her breath, hoping that the interview was over and that she would retain her position.

"Very well," the dowager said at last. "I believe that is all the questions that I have for you at this time. I shall summon the children so that you can meet them."

Sophia's smile was more relaxed as she exhaled with relief.

"That sounds lovely," she said.

As the dowager motioned for a servant to fetch her new charges, Sophia sat in silence. The day already felt as though it had been a fortnight long, and it was not even yet noon. She wondered if she would need to begin lessons that day, even though it was later than tutoring would normally begin. She also wondered about what Mrs. Abernathy had said. She had not wanted to believe gossip. But now, she thought she could see what kinds of challenges she might face as an employee at Rollins Manor.

When Rebecca entered, chaperoning two young children, Sophia rose. She was smiling warmly at her new charges even before the dowager left her seat and reached her hands out toward her grandchildren.

"Thank you, Rebecca," she said, waving her hand toward the young red-headed woman. "I shall call for you when we have finished here."

The woman curtseyed, backing up toward the door. Sophia thought she might have disappeared if she herself had not watched her slip into the shadow of a coat rack.

"My darlings," the dowager said, gushing like any proud grandmother might. "Come, stand with me to meet your new governess, Miss Sophia Hartley."

Sophia took her cue, stepping forward and kneeling primly beside Lady Rollins. She rested her hands casually against her thighs, offering the children eye contact with her.

"It is so wonderful to meet both of you," she said. "Can you tell me your names?"

The dowager glanced at her, and Sophia could not tell whether she was impressed or taken aback. But she did not get time to ponder the expression as the little boy, clearly the older one, stepped forward.

"My name is Henry," he said. He spoke politely, but it was clear that he was reserved. "I am nine years old."

Sophia nodded, holding out her hand for the boy. He looked at it tentatively before giving it one single, light shake.

"It is a pleasure to meet you, Master Henry," she said

warmly, repeating her previous pleasantry.

There was a pause while the girl stared down at her feet. After a moment, Henry nudged his sister, whispering something to her that Sophia could not hear. The dowager watched closely, her lips pursed, and Sophia feared that she would scold the child. She was just about to initiate the introduction with the girl herself when she finally took half a step away from her brother.

"My name is Elizabeth," she said, keeping her eyes on the floor. "I am seven."

Sophia had to strain to hear her. But she did just as she had with Henry and offered her hand. The girl put a finger in her mouth and stepped back, turning her face away from Sophia. It saddened Sophia to see such young children so burdened and wary. But she held fast to the warmth she wished for them to feel and smiled sweetly at the girl, even though she was no longer looking at Sophia.

"It is wonderful to meet you as well, Miss Elizabeth," she said. "I would like to know all about your favourite subjects. Perhaps, we can discuss those when we begin our lessons."

Henry looked dubious, but he nodded. Something in his eyes made Sophia's heart ache further. He clearly wanted to connect and engage. But something was stopping him. Were even the children afraid to open up to their father and grandmother?

"That will be all, Rebecca," the dowager said matter-of-factly.

Rebecca nodded, hurrying over to the children, and ushering them out of the room. Sophia was surprised by the abrupt end to the meeting, but she tried not to let it show.

Once the children were well out of sight, the dowager turned to Sophia once more.

"That went well enough," she said. She was polite, but there was a dismissive edge to her voice, as though she was losing interest in the interaction. "You may go. Lessons will begin first thing tomorrow morning. Eight o'clock precisely. Tardiness will not be accepted."

Sophia nodded, forcing herself to give the dowager another polite smile.

"I understand," she said with a respectful curtsey. "I look forward to it."

Lady Rollins nodded, but did not say another word. Sophia turned and left the room, trying not to flee as if for her life. The children, although aloof and shy, had been pleasant. She suspected they would make wonderful charges. The dowager, however, made Sophia nervous. It was apparent that she had a difficult road ahead of her. But she knew she had to make it work, no matter what.

As she made her way back to her room, careful not to get herself lost along the maze of hallways, she nearly bumped straight into Mrs. Barnes. Sophia gasped, stepping back and preparing for another sharp remark from the housekeeper.

"Miss Hartley," the woman said, her cool eyes searching her face. Something there must have softened her because she gave Sophia a small but warm smile. "I trust Lady Rollins explained to you when lessons begin."

Sophia nodded, trying to suppress her nerves.

"Yes, she did," she said. "Eight o'clock precisely."

Mrs. Barnes nodded, her eyes warming along with her smile.

"Yes," she said. "The nursemaid, Rebecca Lane, will speak with you tomorrow morning and tell you anything you need to know before your first lessons." The housekeeper glanced around, moving to put a gentle arm around Sophia. The change in the woman's demeanor startled Sophia, but she was grateful for the kindness, however sudden. "And it is best that you always be on time. If you are ill, you must let Miss Lane or me know immediately. And we must do everything we can to get you on the lessons as quickly as possible."

Sophia nodded, but her mind reeled. Did the Rollins family not make allowances for their employees falling ill?

"I understand," she said as she had to the dowager.

Mrs. Barnes nodded again, but her brow furrowed. Then, she smiled again, one that lit up her entire face.

"Forgive my earlier abruptness," she said. "I am always wary of new employees. Not everyone comes here with pure intentions, I can assure you. But I see that I was mistaken about you. The pallor of your face and the fear in your eyes is more than enough evidence of that. I assure you, Miss Hartley, everything will be fine here. It is an adjustment, but you will do well, so long as you perform your duties precisely as expected."

Sophia exhaled, allowing relief to take over. But a caution in Mrs. Barnes' eyes made her hesitate. She mulled over the primary concern in her mind, wishing to choose her words as carefully as possible.

"I intend to never do anything to cross Lord and Lady Rollins," she said. "However, I do worry that my tenure here could be ended at a moment's notice."

Mrs. Barnes' eyes filled with understanding. Though her overall expression did not change, she gave the most imperceptible nod.

"Everything will be just fine," she repeated, her voice low and filled with warning. "All you must do is focus on your duties. And whatever you do, do not draw undue attention to yourself. Lady Rollins has high expectations. Although they are not impossible, she does not bend on them. And Lord Rollins is... a bit distant and removed from the goings on within the manor. We rarely see him, unless there is urgent need to speak with one of us."

Sophia understood that the housekeeper meant that he did not speak with employees unless it was in regard to their performance or employment. The information did little to reassure her. But the new kindness in Mrs. Barnes' eyes did. It made her feel as though there was someone who understood how she felt and wanted to help her adjust. Things might be difficult at first. But she had to believe that it would get easier as she found her routine at Rollins Manor.

"Thank you for telling me these things," she said, giving the housekeeper a kind smile. "All I want is to prove myself to Lord and Lady Rollins and give the children the best education I can manage. I would never wish to make trouble or jeopardise my position in any way."

Mrs. Barnes nodded, giving her the kindest smile yet.

"I believe that now, dear," she said. "And again, I do apologise for being so harsh with you previously."

Sophia smiled and shook her head.

"Think nothing of it," she said. "I can understand you being so protective of the Rollins family."

Mrs. Barnes nodded. She looked as though she wanted to say something more, but eventually decided against it. She smiled once more, giving Sophia a nod.

"You should get to your room and rest," she said. "Tomorrow will be here before you know it. And I must return to my duties. But please, let me know if you need anything."

Sophia nodded, waving as the housekeeper walked away. Then, she went to her room, closing the door firmly behind her. Once she was alone, she allowed herself to process the events that had just unfolded. The most puzzling encounter by far had been that with the viscount. Lord Rollins had been largely polite. But there had been a certain tension in his presence that she had never experienced in her twenty years of life. And he had departed from the interview, which she would have believed was especially important to him since it directly involved his children, as though there could possibly be something more important than they were to him. It was strange, to say the least. And it left Sophia with so many questions about her new employer.

That is not my concern, she scolded herself, shaking her head. I am here to educate and care for the children. It is not up to me to figure out a strange, icy viscount. I must concentrate on my duties, like Mrs. Barnes said. Mother and Lucy count on it.

She sighed, thinking of her mother and sister. She prayed that they would be well without her. She knew that the successful retention of her position was critical to creating a stable financial future for her family. The Rollins children were her main priority, indeed. But they were such because Sophia's mother and sister were the overall priority. She should never forget that.

She glanced at the locket with her father's picture and smiled. She missed him dearly, and she would do anything to make him proud. She promised herself that she would put all her concentration and dedication into her new position. Nothing would ever become more important to her than that. No matter what.

Chapter Eight

Sophia had not expected to sleep after the nerve-wracking interview with Lord and Lady Rollins and the anxious energy with which she had retired the previous evening. But before she knew it, she was waking at just before seven in the morning on her very first day as governess. She jumped out of bed, dressing in her plain gray uniform. She was surprised at how rough and abrasive the material felt against her skin. She and her mother and sister had grown accustomed to linen clothing. But the uniform felt as though it had been made with wool from sheep that had been used to scrub floors.

She washed her face and hands quickly in the washroom at the end of the second-floor hallway. Then, she tied back her hair into a neat bun. It was a style to which she was accustomed, as she had often done her hair in such a fashion when helping her mother with the seamstress work. It took her a surprisingly short amount of time to get ready for the day. And yet, by the time she was dressed and looking presentable, she was late for breakfast.

No matter, she thought as she left the washroom. There is not any time to eat just now, anyway. And that was perfectly fine with her. In truth, she was too nervous to eat. Even if she had had two more hours in which to do so. She decided to head to the nursery, thinking to help finish the children get ready for the day. She knew that Rebecca was their nursemaid. But if she could prove that she would take initiative and be beyond punctual, perhaps she could more permanently secure her position at Rollins Manor.

Rebecca started when Sophia knocked on the door. The nursemaid already looked frazzled, and the day had only just begun. She was smoothing out a wrinkle in the apron of a pink dress on a little girl who appeared to be about seven years old. The girl was unmoving. But Sophia soon saw that was the entire problem. She stood as though afraid to move, perfectly stiff and forcing Rebecca to do everything to help her dress, including turning her little body so that her nursemaid could finish straightening her outfit.

"Good morning, Miss Hartley," Rebecca said, sounding breathless.

Sophia smiled, reaching for the girl, and helping finish turning her so that Rebecca could complete her morning task.

"Good morning, Rebecca," she said. "Do you need help with anything before lessons begin?"

The nursemaid shook her head, knocking a curly tuft of red hair loose from her bun. She blew it away from her gray eyes with frustration, giving Sophia a sheepish smile.

"No, they are dressed now," she said. "However, Lord Rollins wanted me to explain Henry's and Elizabeth's routine to you before you begin."

Sophia nodded. She should have been relieved to have some structure to her lessons. But hearing that the viscount had specifically ordered that she learn a routine, made her feel more nervous than ever before.

"Very well," she said, offering the nursemaid another smile. "I shall be happy to adhere to any routine that Lord Rollins wishes."

Rebecca looked doubtful and reluctant, but she nodded.

"The first lesson of the day is always arithmetic," she said. "He wants to ensure that no matter what happens throughout the day, the children never miss any arithmetic. The next is penmanship, as he considers those to be the two most important lessons."

Sophia nodded, committing everything to memory as quickly as she could. She wished she had had a way to write everything down as the nursemaid was telling it to her. But surely, she could remember a few educational lessons on her own. Could she not?

"The viscount does not usually mind if the children take a lesson or two outside once in a while," she said. Sophia noticed only then that the nursemaid sounded just as friendly as she had the day before, but every word she spoke was tinged with caution and a nervousness that Sophia was coming to recognize. She bit her lip before continuing. "However, he does not like for the children to spend too much time distracted from the primary goal of their lessons, which is, of course, to educate them as well as

65

possible."

Sophia nodded again, sparing a glance at the children. They were sitting at small desks in the nursery, which Sophia found odd.

"Do they not have their lessons in a schoolroom?" she asked.

Rebecca shook her head almost apologetically.

"They have a schoolroom," she said, still sounding careful with her words. "However, it has not yet been finished. The governesses have just done lessons in here until Lord Rollins chooses to finish it."

Sophia nodded, wondering how much of her day she would spend repeating that action.

"I see," she said, brightening her smile. "Well, I believe that I am ready to begin if the children are."

Rebecca glanced nervously at the children before turning back to Sophia.

"Very well," she said, sounding uncertain as to whether she believed Sophia. "Do let me know if they need anything. Do not hesitate. Best that I help you before the viscount and the dowager discover that you need help with anything."

Sophia started to nod yet again, but the nursemaid quickly excused herself and exited the room. Sophia bit her lip. What was it about the viscount and the dowager viscountess that made everyone so nervous? And did Sophia want to find out for herself?

Once Rebecca left, Sophia turned back to the children. They were sitting in their seats, staring straight ahead at the blackboard at the front of the room. Sophia approached the board, smiling warmly at the children once more.

"Are the two of you ready to begin your arithmetic lessons for today?" she asked.

The children nodded in unison, but neither of them said anything. Sophia supposed she could understand. They had only just met her, and according to everything she knew, they had had many governesses. It made sense that they were wary. She would just have to do her best to ease their worry.

"As you learned yesterday, my name is Sophia Hartley," she said as she wrote a basic addition problem on the board. "The two of you are my very first charges, and I am delighted to get to know both of you."

Henry kept his eyes on Sophia as she talked. Elizabeth, however, looked down at her desk, as motionless as she was emotionless. Henry looked as though there was something he wished to say. But when remained silent, Sophia took it upon herself to try again.

"Before we begin the arithmetic lesson, I would love to know more about you," she said. "What are some of your favourite things to do?"

Henry and Elizabeth exchanged looks. Sophia bit her lip, hoping the children would open up to her. And when Elizabeth spoke, she thought she had succeeded.

"I like art," she said.

Sophia grinned.

"Wonderful," she said. "I also enjoy art. What do you like to paint or draw?"

Elizabeth looked away again and shrugged, keeping her shoulders up around her ears.

"Animals, I suppose," she said. She sounded very polite, but equally as uncertain, as though she had only said what she felt she should say. Still, Sophia was not willing to criticize her words. She decided that she would show support to anything the children shared with her, to show them that she always would.

"Creating art with images of animals is wonderful, is it not?" she asked. Then, she turned her smiling face onto Henry. "And you, Henry? Do you like art?"

Henry shrugged. He was looking directly at Sophia, but his eyes were guarded and cautious.

"Sometimes," he said. "I suppose I like to sketch once in a while."

Sophia nodded, sighing inwardly. The children, while completely respectful, were very wary. Whether it was just of her or of everyone in their lives, she could not be certain. What she did know was that she needed to do something to try to change that. So, after an hour of arithmetic and penmanship lessons, she erased the blackboard and smiled at the children once more.

"You two have done very well," she said. In truth, the

children had barely spoken two words each to her. They had, in fact, done little except for look at their papers as they were writing. They refused to give her anything more than polite responses to her questions, rendering her unable to connect with them.

The children nodded, glancing at each other and shifting uncomfortably in their seats. They seemed restless, as though each minute they spent inside the nursery made them more ill at ease. She made up her mind to do something that she likely should not do on her first day. But she was determined to offer Henry and Elizabeth a safe and nurturing environment.

"What if we were to take a walk through the gardens?" she asked. "I could certainly use a break before we continue. What about the two of you?"

The children looked at each other once more, cautiously hopeful. It was the brightest Sophia had seen their faces, and she was thrilled. Henry was the one to meet her gaze as he nodded carefully.

"That sounds nice," he said. "Will Father approve?"

Sophia smiled again, glad for the small and indirect admission of the boy's concerns.

"He certainly will," she said. "He told me during my interview that we may take walks through the gardens from time to time."

Henry's expression was dubious, but he nodded.

"All right," he said. He paused, looking at his sister, who mimicked his nod. Then, he looked back at Sophia, offering a timid smile. "We would love to go for a walk."

Sophia clapped her hands together, trying to temper her excitement at the tiny victory.

"Splendid," she said. "I am ready when the two of you are."

The children shared one more glance. Then, Henry rose, putting his hand out to his younger sister. Sophia marveled at the affection between the two children and the protectiveness that Henry clearly felt for his little sister. He led her from her seat and over to the door, where Sophia met them to lead them down the stairs and out the back door of the mansion.

Sophia was amazed at the beauty of the gardens. She had

never seen so many different species of roses, lilies, tulips, dahlias and carnations, apart from in books. Each immaculately tended shrub seemed to be color and species specific, carefully arranged and organized for flora lovers, no matter what their favorite flowers were. It was the first time she was seeing the Rollins Manor gardens. But as she glanced at the children, it was almost as if it was their first time, as well.

She took advantage of the opportunity as they pointed and talked excitedly amongst themselves.

"This is a beautiful garden," she said. "I have never seen anything quite like this. Do you two have flowers you enjoy most?"

This time, Henry's smile was bordering on genuine. He looked at Sophia, pointing to a cluster of shrubs that were a pathway over from where they stood.

"I really like the smell of the gardenias," he said. "The smell reminds me of spring rain."

Sophia's heart skipped. The boy was slowly letting down his guard. She would do anything to foster that effort.

"I absolutely agree with you, Henry," she said, beaming. "I used to have a gardenia bush outside my window. My chambers were on the second story of my family's home, but I could smell them so strongly, especially after a good rain."

Henry smiled, his eyes flickering briefly with understanding.

"Do they only come in white?" he asked.

Sophia's heart leapt. It was the first question Henry had asked her all day, even when she could see him mulling over his mathematics problems. She guided them to the bushes, pointing out the rows of gardenia flowers on either side of them.

"White is the most common," she said, gesturing to her left. "However, there are also ivory ones." She paused, pointing to her right. "The fragrances are almost identical, although I have noticed that the ivory ones smell just a little sweeter, while the white ones have a scent that carries further."

Henry walked to one shrub and drew in a deep breath. Then, he walked over to the other. He turned to Sophia and his sister, smiling widely.

"You are right," he said, motioning for his sister to join him.

"Come and see, Elizabeth."

The little girl hurried over to her brother's side, copying his smell intaking. Then, she smiled shyly up at Henry and nodded.

"I like the yellow ones best," she said.

Henry held up his finger, glancing cautiously at Sophia.

"Those are ivory," he said. "Not yellow."

Elizabeth nodded. Though she looked confused, she also appeared eager to please her older brother.

"Ivory," she echoed.

Encouraged by the progress they were making, Sophia put a hand on Elizabeth's shoulder.

"What about you, Elizabeth?" she asked. "Do you have a favourite flower?"

Elizabeth pulled away from Sophia's hand. But when she looked back up at her new governess, there was a sweet smile on her face.

"I like lilies," she said.

Sophia's heart skipped again, and she quickly led them to the rows of lilies.

"Can you show me your favourite ones?" she asked.

Elizabeth hesitated, and Sophia held her breath. Henry remained beside his sister, but he glanced at Sophia and gave her another tentative smile.

After a long moment, Elizabeth pointed. She turned to look at Sophia over her shoulder and a shy smile crept across her face.

"I love the orange ones," she said.

Sophia nearly leapt for joy. Witnessing the children lower their guard with her was the most delightful experience she had had since before her father died.

"Those are incredibly beautiful," she said. "Do you ever get to have orange lilies in the nursery?"

Elizabeth nodded.

"Rebecca comes out here and brings me some sometimes," she said. The very mention of her favorite flowers seemed to inject enthusiasm into the girl's words, and Sophia was impressed.

"What about gardenias?" she asked, looking at Henry. "Do you get to have those in there, as well?"

Henry nodded, grinning once again.

"She brings us flowers once a week," he said. "Mine sit in a vase right beside my bed. They help me sleep."

Sophia nodded, her smile so wide it could have reached her ears.

"That is wonderful," she said. "Is there anything else you like about the gardens?"

The children shared another look, this time with knowing smiles and matching eye sparkles. They nodded, both turning back to Sophia simultaneously.

"We used to love playing hide-and-seek out here," Henry said. "I always excelled in the role of pursuer.'"

Elizabeth briefly came completely out of her shell for a short moment. She put her hands on her hips and looked at her brother with narrowed eyes and lips that threatened to burst into a full smile.

"You were not," she said. "I was. Rebecca even said so."

Henry shook his head, pointing out into the distance at something Sophia did not yet see."

"That is not true, Sister," he said matter-of-factly. Then, he looked at Sophia. "Elizabeth got very lucky one day, following my muddy footsteps to the stables. Rebecca praised her on being clever enough to find my footprints."

Elizabeth lifted her chin proudly, undeterred by her brother's words.

"It was clever," she said. "And after that, I learned how to be more clever when seeking you."

Sophia started to correct the girl on her grammar. But the children sounded so happy and free, unlike she had witnessed up until that point. She decided that was not the time for a grammar lesson. She would just join in the story sharing and try to build a rapport with them.

"My sister and I used to adore playing hide-and-seek," she said, smiling fondly at the memory. "It was difficult to admit, but thinking back, I believe she was the better seeker, once she reached the age of eight."

The children giggled. Elizabeth fell quiet again, but she was smiling and blushing. Henry tilted his head curiously.

"Is your sister older or younger than you?" he asked. "And what is her name?"

Sophia sighed, thinking wistfully of her sister.

"Her name is Lucy," she said. "And she is twelve."

The children's eyes widened, no doubt thinking that the eight year age difference between Sophia and Lucy was more like a whole lifetime. Henry looked at Elizabeth, then at the governess again.

"She is much younger," he said. "Elizabeth is only two years younger than me."

Sophia nodded.

"That was very good subtraction," she said, taking the chance to inject some praise into the conversation. "And yes, eight years is quite a few. But we adore each other very much. I am very lucky to have such a terrific sister."

Henry nodded, looking down at Elizabeth, who was now playing with one of the orange lilies. He opened his mouth to say something. But a rustling behind them drew all their attention. Sophia's heart stopped when she saw the source of the sound. Lord Rollins stood there, watching them with a curious expression on his face. He stood upright when he met Sophia's eyes, his own cooling into impassiveness. No one spoke for a couple of moments. However, Sophia noticed that the children immediately reverted back to their reserved, quite states.

Feeling at a loss, she stepped forward, closer to the children. She smiled down at them as fondly as she had when she was thinking about her sister, praying that they were not already lost to her again.

"Why don't you go and greet your father, children?" she asked.

Henry and Elizabeth looked up at her, then quickly looked away. She glanced up at the viscount, who was looking at his children. He looked as uncertain as she felt, and she wondered what she should do. It was clear that the viscount was uncomfortable, even with his own children. It was also apparent that the children were desperate for their father's attention and love. How should she handle the situation?

Chapter Nine

Julian avoided leaving his chambers until well after he knew the children should have started their lessons. His mother would have already departed for her weekly shopping trip, and there was no chance that he would encounter any servants. But even as he made his way down the stairs, he had no intention of going straight to his study. Instead, he wanted to walk through the gardens. He had done nothing but review estate bills and ledgers since his interview with the governess. And now, he could think of nothing else. Even as he knew he should be preparing for two business meetings the following week.

It had taken him several months after Eliza's death to traverse the gardens again. It was one of her favorite past times, especially once the children were born. But once he was finally able to walk through the roses and lilies again, he found it often helped him clear his mind. It was not something he did often, as he knew he could hardly afford such distractions. But that day, he thought the fresh air would do him some good.

The sky was beautiful, and birds he could not see were singing in hedges on the outskirts of the gardens. The fragrances from Eliza's favorite roses filled the air and the lilies that lined the bushes leading to the different rows of roses grazed the sleeves of his typical black suit. It was somewhat comforting. But Julian could never truly forget the pressures of his duties. And the more he looked up at it, the more the sky reminded him of the eyes of the new governess.

He shook his head, putting his hands in his coat pocket. He could hardly believe that Miss Hartley had crossed his mind at all after he left her presence. And yet, even as he worked to sort through the figures from his estate ledgers, he thought about her smile and the freckles across her nose and cheeks. It was no longer merely her youth that shocked him. She was every bit as lovely as any noblewoman. Julian thought she might compete with any season's diamond. But why could he not stop thinking about her loveliness? His heart still belonged to his late Eliza. Why did the governess keep coming to mind?

A familiar voice with an unfamiliar sing-song tone pierced his thoughts. His heart jumped into his throat, and he froze. Following that musical voice were two smaller, equally familiar voices. Julian found his feet moving him toward their voices before he could regain control of his thoughts. He found them in a small circular clearing in the gardens, in the midst of some pink roses.

The new governess was telling a story about hide-and-seek and the children were giggling. Julian was once again frozen where he stood as he watched. Miss Hartley was smiling, a real, genuine smile as she talked about metamorphosis and cocoons. The children were smiling, and it appeared as though Henry was about to ask a question. That was until a leaf crunched beneath Julian's heel.

All three of them looked up to see Julian standing there. The smiles immediately melted, and the color drained from Miss Hartley's face. The children instantly fell quiet, casting their eyes to the ground. The silence was more jarring than the sound of their laughter had been to him. It weighted the air infinitely more, as well. Julian might have turned and hurried back toward the mansion, had his feet complied with his brain's desire to do so.

Then tense silence stretched on for so long that perspiration dampened Julian's forehead. He resisted the urge to wipe it away, wishing that someone would break the unsettling quiet. They could not have stood there looking at one another for more than a moment or two, but to Julian, it might as well have been a whole day. The governess spoke to the children, but at first, Julian did not understand what she had said. He only knew that the children looked up at her briefly, almost as if afraid, before looking down at the ground again.

"Children," Miss Hartley said with the softest, most motherly tone. "I implore you, go and offer your salutations to your father. It is completely permissible, I assure you."

Henry and Elizabeth glanced over their shoulders, which were hunched up around their ears, at the new governess once again. Their expressions were those of matching uncertainty. Julian shifted uncomfortably, wondering what Miss Hartley would do. She merely smiled, however and bent down to meet the children's eyes closely.

"Go on, Henry," she said, patting the boy's back with a gentle hand. "You and your sister should say hello to your father. It is very rude to ignore someone who has entered the space you occupy. Especially your own father."

He watched the way the governess interacted with his children. It was long gone upon his arrival, but it had been clear to him that Miss Hartley had managed to bring out something in the two of them that he had not seen in years. She had been encouraging and kind, even something like loving when speaking to the children. And they were responding to her, even though more tentatively as he stood watching them. Something he could not decipher flitted through his emotions. He wanted to speak, but he could not make his mouth form any words. He tried to keep his expression neutral, hoping he did not look as lost as he felt.

Henry turned back toward Julian, who did not realize he was holding his breath until right then. The boy took Elizabeth's hand and together, they reluctantly approached Julian.

"Good day, Father," Henry said, aiming his chin away from the ground. Yet despite the confidence indicated by the gesture, his eyes were filled with doubt and fear.

Elizabeth looked at her brother and, although she only watched Julian through her lashes, she gave him a tiny curtsey.

"Good day, Papa," she said. There was longing in her voice and her eyes, and Julian was filled with guilt. Only in that moment did he understand the true extent of the emotional distance that had developed between his children and him. And it was all his fault.

Julian tried to smile at his children, succeeding only in twitching the corners of his lips as he nodded his head.

"Good day, children," he said. He was angry with himself with the cool response. But how could he be expected to be so open with the children he was supposed to be raising with his beloved Eliza?

Unable to bear the reluctance and sadness in his children's

eyes, he quickly looked at the governess. She had been watching the children with patience and concern. But when she felt her employer watching her, she met his gaze. Her eyes widened, and she curtseyed.

"In teaching them manners, I seem to have forgotten mine, my lord," she said. "Please, forgive me. Good day, Lord Rollins."

Julian nodded slowly, studying her carefully.

"I understand that I granted permission for you to host lessons outside," he said. "It was an inspired choice to do so for their very first ones with you."

Miss Hartley looked flustered, but only for the briefest of moments. She collected herself with a speed that was most astonishing. He raised an eyebrow unconsciously as she spoke.

"I feel that it is important for the children and I to learn about one another," she said. "We completed both the arithmetic and penmanship lessons for the day, and I thought that we could do a brief unit about flowers to learn something new about each other."

Julian nodded. He could not say as much out loud, but the new governess was impressing him, even with her decision to take the children outside on her very first day. He had meant that they could have lessons outside once a month or so. But he did not feel the urge to correct her. Not after having seen the way the children acted with her.

"I trust that lessons went well, then?" he asked.

Miss Hartley smiled warmly at the children again as she nodded.

"Everything went very well," she said. "Elizabeth and Henry both did perfectly with their assignments. That is the other reason why I thought I would treat them with a lesson outside."

Julian nodded again. He would normally have reminded a governess of her place in the manor, pointing out that while she had certain permissions, she should not overuse them. However, when he looked at Miss Hartley, he could not bring the words to his lips.

"And what is it that you have learned?" he asked. "About one another, that is."

Miss Hartley's face lit up as she gazed at the children again.

"I discovered that Henry's favourite flowers are both white and ivory gardenias, and that Elizabeth's is the orange lily." She gasped, pausing as she looked at the children apologetically. "I forgot to tell you my favourite flower. Mine is the pink rose."

The children, temporarily forgetting their father's presence, turned to the governess again.

"Those are pretty," Elizabeth said. She spoke softly, but her eyes gazed at the governess with a look of flitting connection.

Henry smiled, his expression breaking from its reserved mask.

"Those smell nice, too," he said. "Not quite as nice as gardenias, but I like to smell them too."

Miss Hartley giggled, and Julian's heart stopped again.

"You are quite right, Henry," she said warmly. "They do not smell quite as sweet as gardenias. But the scent makes a lovely perfume, and I adore that."

The children nodded. Then, as Miss Hartley glanced back up at Julian, they seemed to remember he was there. They fell silent once more and cast their eyes to the ground yet again. But Julian was enraptured with the governess's poise and the true affection she showed to Henry and Elizabeth. It was unlike anything he had ever seen, and it was as intoxicating as her beauty.

What are you thinking, you fool? He wondered, silently scolding himself. *There is nothing appropriate about what you are thinking. She is the governess. She is an employee. Your employee. Nothing is worth forfeiting the proper distance one is to keep from one's employees.*

"Well, I am glad to see that you are adhering to the rules thus far," Julian said, breaking the silence and the spell the governess seemed to be weaving over him. "Be sure to keep it that way, Miss Hartley. Now, if you will excuse me, I am afraid that I must be going. Good day."

With a curt nod, careful to avoid eye contact with the governess and the children, Julian turned and headed back the way he came. Only he did not go back toward the mansion. Instead, he wove his way to the far left corner of the gardens, unable to bring himself to concentrate on business right away. He was fighting with the feelings the governess seemed to have awakened within him. It was wonderful that the children were responding so well to her, especially so soon. But he felt a strong developing attraction to her, which filled him with terrible guilt. He could not forget his duties as viscount, and he had no business even entertaining the thoughts he was having. But he was sure that Miss Hartley would continue to rattle him in ways he could not even begin to consider or admit, even to himself.

Eventually, he dragged himself back to the manor. He was no more ready to begin work for the day, but he could not risk encountering the governess in the gardens again. He could not risk running into her on accident even. And he had to do whatever he could to ensure that. He would go to great lengths to keep an appropriate distance between the governess and himself. Boundaries must exist in their professional relationship, and he was aware of that. It was up to him to enforce those boundaries. And he would do precisely that.

Chapter Ten

Sophia awoke the following morning eager to don her simple gray uniform. The previous day's encounter with Lord Rollins in the gardens had shown her something critical about the children. They desperately wanted to open up and connect with the people and the world around them. But even they found their father cool and unapproachable. She thought again about what Mrs. Abernathy had said about the viscount's reputation. But she pushed the thought aside immediately. His demeanor was not her job. At least, not exactly. The children and their love for education were.

As she twisted her hair into the bun which had become her quick, easy morning style, she thought about how excited the children had been over the butterfly. She recalled what Rebecca had said about Lord Rollins not having any problem with the children taking some lessons outside. And while she did not wish to anger him by abusing that rule, she also knew that she would need a way to remain connected to Henry and Elizabeth so that she could keep them engaged with learning. That would likely mean as many trips to the gardens as she could manage. She just needed to figure out how to host legitimate lessons outdoors as often as possible.

Determined to continue making progress with the children as she had in the brief period before they encountered the viscount, Sophia finished getting ready for the day and hurried from her room. She headed straight for the nursery, where Henry and Elizabeth were already playing quietly in the corner. Rebecca had already gone, but that was fine with Sophia. She liked the nursemaid, and hoped they could become friends. But the young woman's nervousness only fed Sophia's. And right then, she needed to be calmer and more confident than she had ever been in her life.

When the children saw that Sophia had entered the room, they gave her tentative but brilliant smiles. Elizabeth even set aside her doll and rose, giving Sophia a small, awkward curtsey.

"Good morning, Miss Hartley," she said.

Sophia returned the children's smile with the biggest, warmest smile she had ever given.

"Good morning, children," she said, nodding to Henry as he rose to begin putting away their toys. "Would you like a few moments to clean up before we begin?"

Both children nodded, and Elizabeth stooped to help her brother pick up the toys.

"Will we be going into the gardens again today?" Henry asked with a wistfulness that a deaf man could hear.

Sophia shrugged innocently.

"I cannot say for sure," she said. "But we can try to get through our other lessons and see if we have time. I am certain the two of you cannot wait to learn more about nature."

Henry and Elizabeth nodded again in unison, their smiles becoming less reluctant and more hopeful.

"I wish to learn more about caterpillars," Henry said, his dark green eyes sparkling. "It is fascinating how they turn into butterflies."

Elizabeth nodded shyly, looking away as though she was almost afraid to speak.

"I thought you seemed very taken with that butterfly, Elizabeth," Sophia said, making sure that she sounded encouraging and interested in what the girl might have to say. "Perhaps, the next time we get to go to the gardens, we can find butterflies that are different colours."

Elizabeth's smile widened just a little.

"I would love to see a yellow one," she said softly.

Sophia nodded, making a mental note of what the girl said.

"We will keep our eyes open for any yellow butterflies, just for you," she said. "And for caterpillars for Henry, as well."

The children seemed thrilled by such prospects, grinning at each other as they scrambled to their seats.

"Well, shall we begin?" Henry asked, folding his hands neatly on his little desk. "The faster we get finished, the faster we can discuss going back outside."

Sophia smiled, her heart swelling.

"That is correct, Henry," she said.

She had no interest in offering them their daily arithmetic lesson that day. She had come up with a plan and she was anxious to set it in motion. She knew that the viscount would be terribly displeased with her if she did not stick strictly to the curriculum, however, so she completed the lesson segment as quickly as she could, breaking down the subject into two parts to fit with the children's proficiency with mathematics.

When it came time for the penmanship lesson, Sophia smiled.

"Today, I would like to combine your penmanship lesson with history," she said.

Henry perked up, his eyes widening.

'Truly?" he asked with a hopeful smile.

Sophia nodded, her smile making her cheeks ache. She could sense that she was making progress with making the lessons less tedious for the children. Eliza did not react as her brother did, but she looked intrigued.

"What will we learn about?" she asked.

Sophia shrugged.

"Start by telling me what the last thing was that you learned about history," she said.

Eliza frowned, her brow furrowing as she thought it over. It was evident to Sophia that she was struggling to remember, and Sophia suspected that history might not have been previously fun for her. Henry, on the other hand, nearly knocked himself out of his seat with the speed with which he raised his hand.

"Miss Davis was explaining what she called The Great Coal Fire," he said. Then, he also frowned. "But I cannot remember when she told us it happened."

Sophia smiled at her success with engaging Henry.

"It was in 1784," she said. "Can you tell me what caused such thick, intense smog?"

Eliza's frown deepened and she shook her head. Henry, however, nodded, waving his hand, which he had yet to lower.

"Fires, correct?" he asked, his eyes pleading to be right. "There was foggy smoke caused by fires, I am sure of it."

Sophia nodded, widening her smile to encourage the boy.

"That is correct," she said. "Can you recall what caused the fires?"

Henry nodded, bobbing his head so fiercely that Sophia feared he might injure his neck.

"It was coal," he said. "Everything was fueled by coal, and the smoke filled the whole city."

Sophia clapped her hands together, still smiling.

"Correct again, Henry," she said. "Can you tell me anything else about England in the late 1700's?"

Henry shook his head, but his eyes lit up brightly.

"Can we learn something today?" he asked.

Sophia giggled, thrilled with the boy's enthusiasm.

"What if we make it a game?" she asked. "I will tell the two of you a major event, and you try to guess some minor events that resulted from the big one."

Elizabeth's expression brightened to match her brother's as they both nodded.

"Yes," they said, almost in unison.

Sophia turned to the blackboard, writing 'American Revolution' on its surface before facing the children again.

"Do either of you know anything about this?" she asked.

Both children shook their heads, but Henry raised his hand.

"What does 'revolution' mean?" he asked.

Sophia pointed to the phrase on the board.

"In this instance, it means a war," she said. "To be exact, a war between Britain and America."

Elizabeth's brow furrowed as she raised her hand.

"What is 'America?'" she asked.

Sophia bit her tongue. Had no one ever mentioned America to them?

"It is a wonderful, different country," she said. "We shall discuss it more as we talk about the revolution. Now, are you ready to begin the game?"

Henry's hand shot up, and he was practically bouncing in his seat.

"In war, rulers change, and lands get conquered," he said.

Sophia beamed at him. He knew nothing about the American Revolution, and yet he had already described a good portion of the results of the war.

"Very good, Henry," she said. "Elizabeth, would you like to take a guess as to something that might have happened during the revolution?"

The girl's brow furrowed as she mulled over the question. Sophia was glad to see her shyness dissolving, giving way to genuine, deep thought.

"People get hurt in war," she said at last.

Sophia nodded, giving her an encouraging smile.

"That is correct, Elizabeth," she said.

The rest of the lesson carried on in such fashion. She even wrote facts down on small pieces of paper while the children covered their eyes and hid them all over the nursery for the children to find with clues she gave them. They were laughing and filled with delight each time they found a new fact. It seemed that Henry, in particular, took great joy out of learning history.

Similarly, when Sophia pulled out an ancient book about plants, Elizabeth's eyes lit up. Sophia recalled what she had said about orange lilies being her favorite flower, and she called Elizabeth to the blackboard.

"Can you draw a lily from memory?" she asked.

Elizabeth stared up at the board, frowning.

"I believe so," she said. "But it will be black."

Sophia laughed.

"It will appear black, that is true," she said. "But we can use our imaginations to pretend that it is any colour you like. Even orange." She gave the little girl a wink.

That seemed to do the trick. Elizabeth took the piece of chalk and began drawing. By the time she was done, Henry was clapping and the girl was smiling more widely than Sophia had ever seen. And on the blackboard was a rather good depiction of a lily.

"There we are," Elizabeth said, pointing at the board with a flourish of her little hands. "My orange lily."

Sophia joined Henry in his applause, smiling warmly at the girl.

"Very well done, Elizabeth," she said. "You enjoy learning all about flowers and other plants, do you not?"

Elizabeth's face brightened as she nodded eagerly.

"It is my favourite thing to learn about," she said.

Sophia gave her a knowing smile. This was a far more honest answer to the question Sophia had asked them on her first day of lessons. She had expected that the children were not being truthful about their true interests, and she was simply grateful that they were opening up enough to be honest with her right then.

"Well, then you are in luck," she said, winking at the girl again. "I was just thinking that we should take a short walk in the gardens, since we have worked so hard all morning."

Both children leapt with excitement, racing to the door as Sophia followed them. She led them straight to the back door, watching with joy as the children bolted out into the sunshine, stretching their small arms toward the sky. It warmed Sophia's heart to see them finally behaving as young, carefree children should. She walked along behind them, taking in the beautiful flowers and a small cluster of butterflies that kept fluttering around the bushes.

Suddenly, there was a small added weight to her right hand. She glanced down to see Elizabeth standing right beside her, with Henry to her left. She also noticed that the little girl had slipped her hand into Sophia's. She was smiling up timidly at Sophia, and the governess understood. She gently squeezed the child's hand and gave her a loving, reassuring smile to let her know that she did not mind the girl seeking comfort and showing trust in such a manner. She fought the tears that filled her eyes as she took a deep breath.

"Shall we go back inside?" she asked. "I imagine it is almost lunch time."

The children agreed. They chatted excitedly as they headed back to the manor. However, Elizabeth did not release Sophia's hand and Henry did not leave her side until they were heading up the stairs to the nursery. Sophia was touched and thrilled by the amount of progress she seemed to be making with the children. And she was so caught up in those thoughts that she gasped when she saw Rebecca in the nursery waiting for them.

"Oh heavens, do forgive me," Rebecca said with a blush when she realized she had startled Sophia. "I merely brought a tray of freshly baked biscuits and tea for the children. I thought they could use a little treat."

Sophia looked down at the heaping plate of biscuits and large pot of steaming tea. She glanced at the nursemaid, giving her a nod of understanding and receiving one in return. The two women shared a moment of recognition, both realizing how important things like unexpected treats and fun adventures outdoors were for children like Henry and Elizabeth.

The children were expectedly thrilled. They rushed to the table on which the tray sat, motioning to Rebecca and Sophia.

"It is a tea party," Elizabeth squealed, patting a small empty space on the table beside her. "Come join us, Miss Hartley."

Henry beamed at the woman who had brought them the treats.

"You join us, too, Miss Lane," he said. "Please?"

Sophia and Rebecca shared another look. They nodded to each other again and then smiled.

"We would love to join you," Sophia said.

The tea party lasted until well into the afternoon. It was not until Rebecca rose and reached for the children's hand that Sophia realized how much time had passed. The children had laughed, talked and shared more stories about their short lives for hours, and for Sophia, it had felt like mere minutes.

"It is nearly time to get them ready for dinner," she said, sounding apologetic.

Sophia nodded, rising from her seat and stifling a yawn. It had been quite an adventurous day, and she did not realize how much energy it had taken from her.

"Very well," she said, kneeling to look the children in the eyes. "I shall see you first thing in the morning."

The children both nodded, giving her the happiest smiles she had ever seen on their faces.

"Have a good evening, Miss Hartley," Henry said, giving her a small bow.

"Good night, Miss Hartley," Elizabeth said, curtseying.

Sophia laughed and returned their formality with her own curtsey.

"Good evening, my dears," she said. "And good evening to you, as well, Rebecca."

The nursemaid nodded, sharing a secret smile with Sophia.

"Good night, Sophia," she said.

Sophia left the nursery, heading straight for her chambers. Her duties were complete for the day, but her mind was still at work. She was amazed and thrilled about how the day had gone. There was still a great deal that she needed to do to help the children get through losing their mother, their aloof father, and the apprehension regarding trusting people. However, after the way the children had been so eager to participate and share with her when she showed just a little compassion and consideration, she was sure she could manage that work and get the children feeling consistently lively and content with life in no time.

Chapter Eleven

"Julian, do you have a moment?" the dowager asked.

Julian was just rising from the breakfast table, and she had not spoken a word throughout the entire meal. In fact, Julian had spent the whole hour sharing a table with his mother thinking about the vow he had made to himself nearly a week prior about the governess. He had done well enough at keeping away from both the gardens and the nursery since his last encounter with Miss Hartley and his children. But he had thought of little else, even forgetting to reply to a letter from a new potential business partner by the deadline two days before.

"Only just," he said, not taking his seat as he met his mother's gaze. "I am very busy today."

The dowager smiled at Julian, and instantly he regretted granting her an audience.

"I received an invitation for Roseanne's ball this weekend," she said. "I do hope you will consider attending."

Julian's jaw clenched reflexively. The duchess of Ashvale was a high-profile member of the ton, and her parties were well known during the London Season each year. However, Julian felt certain that his mother was not looking to attend because of the prestige. Not if she had waited until practically the last minute to even mention it to Julian.

"I hardly have time to prepare for a ball with just two days' notice, Mother," he said.

Augusta shrugged, still smiling.

"We can have you a suit tailored by the end of the day, if it is necessary, darling," she said with a honeyed voice. "And she and I are well enough acquainted that she will consider our acceptance, even if it is a little late."

Julian bit his tongue to keep from snorting. If Lady Ashvale and his mother were acquainted, that was all they were. And he knew that nobility accepted invitation replies until the day before the ball. He was sure he knew what his mother was doing. And yet he also knew that he would not be leaving the table until he agreed to attend the ball with her.

"Very well," he said curtly. "I shall escort you. But having a suit tailored will not be necessary. And I do not have time."

The dowager's smile widened, and he knew she did not hear what he had said. She had gotten what she wanted. And Julian knew he would regret it.

"Thank you, darling," she said. "I shall not bother you while you work. Be ready at six o'clock on Saturday evening. Roseanne hosts the loveliest balls. You shall not regret this."

Julian stifled a groan as he left the room without a word. I am certain that I shall, he thought.

That Saturday, Julian dressed in yet another of his black suits. He felt sure that his mother would comment on the lack of interest in his wardrobe when she met him at the bottom of the grand staircase wearing a fine silk purple evening gown. But she simply smiled at him, kissing him on both cheeks.

"This will be a wonderful evening, Julian," she said.

Julian dipped his head, resisting the urge to shake it. I am certain it will not...

Ashvale Estate was vast and colorful, from the entrance of the carriage-way to the entrance to the grand ballroom. Bright hues of yellow, pink, green, orange and purple assaulted his eyes as he escorted his mother into the room already filled with chattering guests. Julian's cold, detached façade was securely set in his mind and on his face, but he still felt terribly uncomfortable. He did his best not to eavesdrop on the shallow conversations around him. But the bits that could be heard over the sounds of the orchestra warming up their instruments reminded him of how hollow and dry he felt inside.

He allowed his mother to lead the two of them through the groups of guests that mingled on the fringes of the ballroom floor. Unlike him, she was darting her eyes all over the room. Julian did not need to guess what she was doing. If she was not searching for ladies whom she believed would be good matches for him, she was looking for one woman in particular. And a moment later, he learned which of the two it was.

Lady Irene stood with her parents at the far-right corner of the dance floor. And the dowager directed Julian and herself toward them with a broad smile. Julian shuddered. He wished he could pull himself away from the unwanted interaction. But with a ballroom full of people, there was no way he could do so without attracting unwanted attention. Although, as Lady Irene greeted Julian with a pretentiously modest curtsey and smile, he wondered if causing a scene might not be less unpleasant after all.

As his mother greeted Lady Irene's parents, the young woman stood watching Julian expectantly through her lashes. Julian sighed. He was trapped, and he knew it. And from the look in her eyes when she glanced up at him, Lady Irene knew it, as well.

"This is a lovely ballroom," he said at last, fumbling to think of polite conversation to strike with Lady Irene.

The young woman looked taken aback that he had not responded differently to her blatant flirtatious behavior. But she kept her smile and nodded.

"Lady Ashvale always chooses the most beautiful themes," she said. "Mother and Father adore her balls for just that reason."

Julian nodded. He doubted very much that any gentleman truly enjoyed brightly themed parties. But then, he also knew that he could not judge the preferences of everyone in the ton based on his own. After all, his preference was to hide behind his study walls and ignore society. What did he know about any social preferences, apart from the expectations of which his mother frequently reminded him?

He was unsurprised to feel eyes on him as he fumbled for more conversation to make with Lady Irene. He was certain that her parents were watching him intently, silently willing him to ask their daughter to dance. He also had no doubt that his mother was of a similar mind, and that her watchful eye was no less intense than that of her peers.

He was equally lacking in shock to see that the nearest other ball guests were looking in their direction. He had no doubt that they were contemplating the odds of him making a match with Lady Irene. He resisted a bitter smirk as he wondered if any of the nosy gentlemen looking curiously at them were interested in the eligible young woman. Would that they would come forward and speak up, he thought with satirical amusement. It would save me a great deal of trouble.

Naturally, no men came forward. In fact, everyone seemed more than content to keep their distance, keeping their gossip and questioning eyes to their own little groups as they continued staring and wondering. Julian ignored them all, though he wished more than ever that he could leave.

However, as the orchestra began to play, his mother touched his arm. It was a quick gesture, but her fingertips squeezed hard enough for him to understand that she was making a deliberate point. He looked down at her to see her smiling. But her eyes were trying to convey a specific message to him.

"Darling," she said, dropping her voice so that only the two of them could hear, despite the close proximity of Lady Irene and her parents. "Why do you not ask Irene to dance?"

Julian's stomach twisted. He had anticipated such a request. But he had hoped that he might escape it if he could just slip away from the young woman without incident. But now that they were speaking in hushed tones, Lord and Lady Locshire were watching with more intrigue than ever before. Julian realized that he had no choice.

"Would you dance with me?" he asked. He was intentionally clipped and curt with his invitation. Yet he was not surprised when Lady Irene giggled and offered her hand.

"I would be most delighted," she said.

Julian sighed, leading the young woman out onto the dance floor. He spoke not a single word as they got into position and began moving in physical harmony across the dance floor. He might be required to dance with the young woman. But there was no such demand that he had to speak to her. Thus, he dismissed any attempts at conversation with curt nods and tight smiles, but nothing more. He did not know when, or if, Lady Irene fell silent. All he knew was that suddenly, his thoughts trickled back to Miss Hartley.

It had been near impossible not to think of her since encountering her in the gardens with the children. He recalled how he had been dubious about her skills, having had no experience, and her age, which was far younger than any governess he had ever seen. He thought about how her beauty had initially caught him so off guard that he had had to leave her presence upon first meeting her. Yet, until those few moments in the gardens, it had been manageable to push her from his mind. Right then, however, he could think of nothing else. Her beautiful smile, the warmth in her laugh and voice as she interacted with the children and the way Henry and Elizabeth looked at her flooded him with deep, intense emotion. He was reminded of how inappropriate it was to have any such thoughts about an employee. But in that moment, he did not care. Those thoughts were precisely where he felt he should be.

He was awash with relief when the dance ended. Lady Irene looked flustered, and Julian did not care. Yet despite her frustration, she still managed to smile coyly at him as he bowed to her at the edge of the dance floor.

"That was a lovely dance," she said, batting her eyelashes at him.

Julian barely swallowed a snort. Her insincerity was just another reason why he would never even think of considering a match with her. It was that falsity and fake manners that disgusted him with the majority of the ton. And it was the reason why he could no longer suffer another moment inside that ballroom.

He grabbed the largest glass of wine he could find, then headed out onto the terrace. He had first hoped to have the space alone, despite being aware that the other ball guests would have the same idea all throughout the night. But when he saw who was currently occupying the space, he grinned.

"George," Julian said, his mood instantly lifting considerably.

His younger brother turned, greeting him with a similar smile.

"Jules, Brother," he said, enveloping Julian in a firm embrace. "How are you enjoying the ball?"

His younger brother snickered as Julian unleashed the eye roll and the heavy exhale of disgusted breath he had been holding in until then.

"Horrible," he said, clapping his younger brother on the back. His mind was still burdened with all his thoughts. But he was very grateful to have his brother for company.

George nodded as he studied his older brother. A moment of silence passed between them before either of them spoke.

"I do wish I had remained at the manor," Julian said with a big sigh.

George nodded again, clapping Julian on the back.

"You have never been one for balls such as this," he said. "I can only guess that this was Mother's doing."

Julian confirmed with a nod.

"It was," he said. "She truly thinks to match me with Lady Irene. The young lady just lied directly to my face. How could Mother ever even entertain the idea of me marrying her?"

George chuckled.

"She could lie directly to Mother's face, and Mother would explain it away if it meant that she had made a match for you," he said.

Julian snorted.

"How right you are, Brother," he said bitterly. "And all the while, it never occurs to her that this might not be what is best for me, or for the children, right now."

George nodded, but his eyes were suddenly filled with concern.

"Jules, I know that Mother should stay out of your affairs with her meddling," he said. "I could not agree more, in fact. But I fear that now, you have closed yourself off to the possibility of ever finding love again merely because Mother pressures you so."

Julian shook his head. He was grateful for his brother's kindness and understanding. But the pressure was not the biggest reason why he avoided matching with any lady.

"Eliza's memory is still so prominent in my mind and my heart," he said. "To even consider remarrying would be to betray her. I simply cannot do such a thing, not when I loved her so dearly."

George's eyes filled with a sympathy that made Julian briefly regret speaking his mind. He lifted his other hand and put it on

Julian's shoulder.

"That is a perfectly valid feeling, Brother," George said softly. "But you must know that Eliza would want you and the children to be happy again. She would want you to open up your heart again to companionship and love."

Julian gave his head another shake, more to shake away the tears than to refuse his brother's words, which he knew carried much truth.

"I cannot," he whispered, wrestling with the emotional typhoon within him. Remarriage meant forgetting his dearest Eliza. And he could never accept such a fate. "I simply cannot."

Chapter Twelve

Sophia had been thrilled when Wyatt brought her the letter from Lucy before lessons. She was tired but pleased with her first week of tutoring the children, and with the progress she had made with getting Henry and Elizabeth to open up to her. However, as she sat in her room reading the letter, her responsibilities as governess were temporarily forgotten. She had longed to hear from home. But what her sister had to say was concerning.

Dearest Sophia,

I hope this letter finds you well. Firstly, I wish for you to know that I miss you dearly, and that I love you more than words can say. Mother sends her love, as well, but it is Mother that I wish to discuss.

Sister, I waited as long as I could to write to you about this. But with each passing day, Mother seems more different than the day before. She is quieter, as though she is always somewhere far away, even as she and I sit and sew in the same room. She has stopped teaching me the stitching you and I were working on before you left and she seems constantly distracted, even as she works. She even looks paler and more tired than she did before, and yet she refuses to tell me what is troubling her.

Perhaps, she is simply missing you more than she says. But even though we just bought more food, she eats less than ever before. She claims to have no appetite, even when I made her favourite chocolate cake last night. I cannot say that I am not overreacting. But I do know that none of this is like Mother, and I am very worried.

Please, write to me as soon as you can. I could use your advice. I adore you, Sister. I very much look forward to hearing word from Rollins Manor.

All my love,
Lucy

Sophia tossed the letter aside. She had half an hour before she was to begin lessons for the day, and she wanted to get her letter to her sister posted before the morning ended. She quickly penned a response, hoping that she could offer her sister the reassurance she clearly needed.

Darling Lucy,

Things are well here. The children are wonderful, and the viscount and dowager viscountess pay me well enough that soon, I shall be able to send you money twice a month, rather than once. I love and miss you and Mother dearly, and I cannot wait until I am able to come and visit.

Dear Lucy, thank you for sharing your concern for Mother. However, I am certain that she is simply struggling to adjust to all the changes. Father has not yet been gone two years, and now I am living away from home and the two of you. Even though it is for the best, I can imagine that it will take some time for Mother to get back to herself. However, keep a close eye on her, and let me know if anything should change any more than it has.

You are a wonderful sister to me, Lucy, and a perfect daughter to Mother. I am so very proud of you, and I am always here for you, no matter how difficult things seem there at home. I feel terrible that the distance between us is so great, and that I cannot be right there to help. But my duty lies with the Rollins children and their education. I am obligated to help them, and I am obligated to make money to take care of you and mother. However, do not hesitate to write any time you feel that you need some help. I will do everything I can for you, sweet little sister, and Mother, as well.

With all the love in my heart,

Sophia

She did not realize until she was sealing up the envelope that she needed the calming words as much as it sounded like Lucy did. It was alarming to receive such news from home, especially with her so far away. But she had to believe that the explanation for their mother's abnormal behavior was a simple as she had told Lucy it was. And she hoped that Lucy would be reassured enough to not worry herself unnecessarily until their mother got back to herself. Which, Sophia was sure, she would.

She glanced at her pocket watch, noticing that it was five

minutes until lessons were to begin. She tucked the letter hurriedly into the pocket of her dress, angry with herself for not leaving enough time to find one of the other staff members and asking them to have Wyatt post it. She hurried to the nursery, where the children were waiting patiently for her, as ever. They smiled sweetly at her as she entered the room, both their eyes filled with curiosity and eagerness.

"Good morning, Miss Hartley," they said in unison. Elizabeth, in a rare moment of outspokenness giggled and waved to Sophia. "You look very pretty today."

Sophia forced a smile. She was still making tenuous progress with the children. That was the first morning they had looked at her with something more than reluctant hope. She could not let her own concerns and stress leave a dark imprint on her responsibilities as Henry's and Elizabeth's governess.

"Good morning, children," she said, allowing herself to laugh a little along with Elizabeth. "Are we ready to begin?"

They nodded, once again in unison.

"We sure are," Elizabeth said.

"I cannot wait to hear more about England's history," Henry said, his eyes sparkling like pale emeralds.

Sophia tried to push aside her worries and allow the children's infectious enthusiasm infect her. She approached the children and gave them both an affectionate pat on the head, struggling to keep her smile.

"I will be delighted to get more into history with you," she said. "However, as we all know, we must get through arithmetic first."

The children made sour faces, but their eyes were still filled with delight. Sophia made her way to the front of the classroom and began the mathematics lesson.

"Miss Hartley?" Henry asked suddenly as she was writing the first set of problems on the blackboard.

"Yes?" Sophia asked, putting on her best pleasant smile.

Henry giggled and pointed.

"You wrote an 'm' in place of the addition symbol," he said.

Sophia turned back to the board, horrified to see that the

young boy was right. She blushed, erasing it, and correcting her mistake.

"Forgive me," she said, smiling as brightly as she could. "What a silly mistake to make. Try it this way."

Henry laughed again, nodding as he looked down at his paper and copying the problems. Elizabeth was already scribbling away, seemingly unbothered by the mistake. The lesson continued without incident, until they reached the end, as Sophia was writing more complex addition problems on the board. She was showing the children how to solve the problems, but they were more distracted than she had been all morning. They were swinging their feet in their chairs, staring out the window and no longer writing on their respective papers.

Ordinarily, she would have tried engaging them with more games to keep them interested. But she kept getting lost in her own thoughts, worrying sick over her mother and concern for Lucy, and she could hardly concentrate herself. She did not feel up to walking through the gardens. However, another idea formed in her mind; one which she was sure would redirect not only her mind, but also the minds of the children.

"I was thinking," she said, trying to sound excited. "Why do we not go to the library today? I am certain that your father has some wonderful history and plant books."

The children needed no convincing. They were running for the door before bothering to answer their governess.

"Oh, yes, let's," Elizabeth said, beaming at Sophia.

The smile melted Sophia's heart, and a small bit of her worry was replaced with delight.

Henry pulled open the door, stepping back so that Sophia and Elizabeth could step through.

"After you, ladies," he said, bowing exaggeratedly.

Sophia laughed as she and Elizabeth complied. Then, she escorted them down the stairs, taking a few deep breaths as they made their way to the library. She hoped that literature could ease her mind and her demeanor. The last thing she wanted was for the children to think they had done something wrong. Ever.

Her troubles were, in fact, temporarily forgotten when they

entered the large library. The mere sight of books felt like a warm embrace, and she entered the room with awe. She approached the nearest shelf, touching one of the books and delighting in the pleasant tingles that ran up her spine.

"You were right, Miss Hartley," Henry gushed, running to a shelf to her left. "There are a bunch of history books here."

Sophia looked at the boy, smiling warmly.

"Feel free to browse them, sweetheart," she said, glad that the boy had found something to hold his interest.

As Henry ran to peruse the history volumes, Elizabeth let out a squeal of delight. She ran to another shelf to Sophia's right, holding up one of them and bouncing up and down.

"Here is a book about lilies," she said, her eyes overflowing with excitement.

Sophia nodded, gesturing toward the shelf.

"See what else there might be, darling," she said.

While the children flipped through book after book, Sophia let her mind wander. She ran her fingers along the spines of the books on the shelf before her, marveling at all the information that surrounded her and taking comfort in such a familiar activity. It had been ages since she had entered a library, and it made her feel more at home than she had felt since arriving at Rollins Manor.

A hair-raising sensation pulled Sophia reluctantly from the warmth that was the solace of the books. Someone was watching her. She glanced at the children, who were still busily turning pages. Then, she turned, finding herself locking eyes with Lord Rollins. Her throat dried and her heart began to race. Had she been wrong in assuming that he would not mind if they turned to the mansion's library for educational literature?

Chapter Thirteen

Julian slept in the morning after Lady Ashvale's ball. He would have had no interest in joining his mother for breakfast even if he had not tossed in bed sleeplessly until after three in the morning. When he finally did wake, the morning sun was already rising toward the highest point in the sky. He summoned Alexander, choosing a dull gray suit for the day. He knew he could not avoid his mother forever, and perhaps, not even until the end of the day. But he cared less about impressing her with his attire than he had cared about dancing with Lady Irene the evening before.

After he dismissed Alexander, Julian tried to decide what to do for the day. He still had papers that required signatures, but he was in no mood to concentrate. And while it was a lovely day for a walk in the gardens, he did not wish to disrupt another of Miss Hartley's lessons with the children. If he was not careful, she might think he was seeking her out on purpose. And as he had the thought, he ignored the part of himself that made him think he might actually be.

After much deliberation, he finally decided to go to the library. It had been ages since he had afforded himself the luxury of reading a good book. And if he was going to spend the day unable to concentrate on his duties, he thought it could do little more harm to enjoy one of his favorite stories.

He slipped quietly out of his chambers and down the stairs, hoping that his mother had given up waiting for him to have breakfast with her and gone about her day. When he made it all the way to the library door without running into her, he felt relieved. He longed for the solace of his books. With any luck, they could succeed in lifting the weight that Julian constantly felt that he wore on his shoulders. Especially since his mother had begun pressuring him about marriage.

He had just turned to close the door when he heard a soft rustle on the other side of the room. He turned, surprised to see

Miss Hartley and the children standing with their backs to him, staring up at one of the shelves. He released the handle to the door immediately, not disappointed when it did not make a sound as it slowly stopped its journey to the doorjamb. He watched as the young governess caressed the spines of the books in front of where she stood with a fondness that was not unlike that which he himself felt for them.

He did not notice when Elizabeth moved to get the governess's attention. He did, however, see that when Miss Hartley turned to look at him, his daughter was holding her hand. He would have felt embarrassed at having sneaked up on the trio. But the instant the governess's eyes met his, he forgot everything except for the specific shade of blue staring back at him.

"Good morning, Lord Rollins," she said, her cheeks turning red as she averted her gaze to curtsey to him.

The children immediately followed suit, bowing and curtseying, respectively.

"Good morning, Father," they said in unison.

Julian was surprised to note that, although their tones remained somewhat reserved, they wore genuine smiles, and they seemed at ease in the library. Specifically, at Miss Hartley's side. Julian silently marveled at the sight, even as he approached the trio with deliberate steps and careful effort to keep his expression unreadable.

"Good morning, Miss Hartley," he said, politely addressing the group in the same order in which they had addressed him. "Good morning, Henry and Elizabeth."

Henry surprised him again by turning to fully face his father, albeit without leaving the new governess's side.

"We came to see if you had any interesting books we could use for our lessons," he said.

Julian's mask slipped as the look of shock crossed his face. He could not recall a time where his children had taken an interest in lessons outside the nursery. Surely, it had been Miss Hartley's idea to bring them to the library.

"Oh?" he asked. "And in what are the children specifically interested in?"

The governess looked down at the children, and Julian could have sworn that he saw fondness in her expression as she did so.

"The children have been learning so quickly from the books in the nursery that we thought we would come and find some new material here," she said. Her words sounded confident, as always, but her voice was soft, as though she was suddenly unsure of herself. "I do hope it is all right that we did so without getting permission first."

Julian shook his head, trying not to wince as he realized what that would mean to them.

"Yes, of course," he said, quick to correct the mixed signals. "This is their home, as well, after all. And yours, Miss Hartley, as you are serving as governess. You are all welcome to come to the library any time you like, especially in the pursuit of education."

Miss Hartley smiled, a small but genuine smile. It lit up her entire face, though briefly, and Julian's heart skipped. It would have been another long moment of staring into eyes that reminded him of a cloudless afternoon sky if Henry had not spoken again.

"I love learning about history, Father," he said, holding up a book on eighteenth century British history. "Did you know that there was once smog so thick that horses could not see but a few inches in front of their noses in London?"

Julian blinked, taken aback for yet a third time.

"I did," he said. He was surprised at his son's memory retention. But he was more shocked by the true interest he heard in Henry's voice as the boy spoke.

Elizabeth gave him a shy look, digging her toe into the carpet beneath her feet as she tightly gripped a book on botany.

"I love plants," she said. "Especially flowers. And I love orange lilies and gardenias most of all."

Julian nodded. That was the most his children had spoken to him all at once in as long as he could remember. And that was the most interested in anything that he had seen them since their mother died. He glanced back up at the governess, who was watching him with a worried expression. When she saw him looking at her again, she corrected her facial features. But there was a lingering emotion in her eyes, something which Julian struggled to identify.

"I realise that we still have literature in the nursery," she said. "And I suspect that there are a few books more in the unfinished schoolroom. However, they are so excited about history and botany that I thought their education would be better served by looking at the very best books in the mansion."

Julian nodded, once more awed by the passion in her voice. She truly did care about the children's interests, and about delivering a strong education to them. He cursed himself for having forgotten about the unfinished schoolroom, having written it off as unimportant after Eliza's death. But he made a mental note to have it finished by the end of that week. He also noted that he needed to find any books on plants and history he could. He might not have offered his children the emotional support they needed for three years. But he could certainly aid in the pursuit of their interests and education.

"And what about you, Miss Hartley?" he asked. "Did you come looking for anything in particular?"

The governess blushed, looking away. It took her a moment, which Julian thought was rather odd for her typical calm, confident demeanor, even with him.

"I do enjoy reading Shakespeare's plays in my free time," she said as uncertainly as she had looked away from him. "I wondered if there might be a book here that held many of them in one tome."

Julian's heart skipped. He, too, enjoyed Shakespeare, although it had been ages since he had attended the theater. A sudden thought gripped him, and he spoke before he could change his mind.

"I believe there is one such book here," he said. "Allow me to help you find it."

Miss Hartley looked as surprised as he felt at his words. He surprised himself further by giving her a small but warm smile. It must have put her somewhat at ease, because she gradually returned the smile, the red deepening in her cheeks and making the sweet freckles on her face stand out.

"That is very kind of you, my lord," she said. "I would very much appreciate that."

Julian dipped his head, marveling at his skipping heart. He had seen that smile on her face, but never directed at him. Why was it having such an effect on him?

He could not quite remember on which case he had placed the book she had referenced. So, he began with the ones with authors whose names began with 'S'. He searched the higher shelves while she looked through the lower ones. They eventually met in the middle, each of them concentrating on their task. He was so focused that he did not realize that she was standing so close to him. Not until his hand brushed against hers as they reached for the same book.

His entire body tingled with awareness, and he completely forgot everything around him for a moment. He was only able to look up at her, finding that she was looking at him, as well. Their eyes met, and his heart stopped. Neither of them could find words and, in that moment, none mattered. He did not understand the feelings coursing through him. But right then, he did not care to try.

The blissfully confusing moment did not last long, however. A sound at the doorway drew Julian's attention and, without moving his hand, he cast a glance in that direction. His mother stood there, shrewdly studying Miss Hartley and her son. With a deliberate smile, she dipped her head at the governess.

"Good day, Miss Harvey," she said. Her condescending eyes told Julian that once again, she had intentionally gotten the young woman's name wrong, and he opened his mouth to correct and reprimand her. But Miss Hartley quickly curtseyed and gave the dowager a polite smile.

"Good day, Lady Rollis," she said, surprising Julian once again. "The children and I were just..."

"That is lovely," she said, looking at Julian before Miss Hartley could finish speaking. "Julian, darling, surely you have not forgotten about teatime. It is crucial that we discuss the ball that Lord and Lady Locshire are hosting this weekend. I do not need to remind you that they are counting on us. And I am counting on you to remember why you are attending."

Julian clenched his jaw, beginning to regret not setting his mother straight again about trying to force him to think of remarrying. But he could not lose his temper in front of the children. He did not wish to frighten or upset Miss Hartley by saying something harsh or rash, either. Thus, he simply nodded. Then, knowing that his mother would not leave the library until he was right on her heels, he turned to the governess and the children.

"Please, excuse me," he said. "I must take my leave. But do browse the books in here as long as you like. And borrow any you feel that you might want or need."

He was looking at Miss Hartley as he spoke. But he spared a glance at his children before turning to leave and giving them a fleeting smile. Then, he walked away, surprised at how heavy his heart was at having to leave the trio. He would have given anything to not have to break that moment of warmth and connection he had felt with Miss Hartley.

Julian followed his mother to the drawing room, where tea and cakes were already waiting for them. They helped themselves, but Julian would have sooner tossed his refreshments into a bin. The unspoken tension and expectations from his mother were thick enough to choke him. He shuffled his treats on his plate, hoping to end the tea as quickly as possible.

"Julian, I am aware that you were displeased with the ball this past weekend," she said. "However, this one is very important. I do not think you realise what image you are projecting to Lord and Lady Locshire. I need you to remember why you are being called to these balls. The one at the Locshire estate, especially."

Julian glanced at his mother just in time to see her pointed gaze. He understood what she was not saying, of course. She was hinting that Lord and Lady Locshire had designs to make him wed Lady Irene. She was also letting him know that they had noticed how uninterested he was. He did not care who was displeased with his lack of desire to court or wed Lady Irene. He had made up his mind. And part of him wanted to reject the ball invitation, no matter what his mother said.

In the end, he simply chose to remain silent and allow his mother to talk. It was just as well, as she had plenty to say.

"Lady Irene truly is lovely," she said. "She has the poise and grace of a duchess. She would make a fine wife, of that, I am sure. And her parents tell me that she is wondrous on the harp. Not to mention how smitten she is with you."

Julian tightened his jaw again, his stomach churning. *She is also an insincere liar, Mother*, he countered silently. As he and George had determined, the dowager likely would not care. But Julian did. He did not want a woman who was boldly trying to pressure him to court her, who lied and threw herself at him, who likely did not even know how to speak to children, let alone how to love them. He wanted someone kind and warm and intelligent. Someone who could easily bond with Henry and Elizabeth. Someone exactly like Miss Hartley.

As he let his thoughts continue, he understood he could not reject the notion that he had felt attraction for the governess. It had been the most pleasant, disorienting moment he had had in years, and part of him wanted nothing more than to repeat that moment time and time again in the future. But the other part of him, the part that had prevented him from exploding on his mother again for her matchmaking attempts, sharply reminded him that no such feelings could exist. He was a viscount. She was a governess. And his family and honor depended on him never forgetting that. No matter what he crazily thought he wanted.

Chapter Fourteen

As the carriage pulled to a stop in front of the Locshire's mansion, Julian's heart was filled with dread. The cream-colored manor was well lit on the first two floors, and everything about the well-manicured lawn and warm glow coming from each of the windows containing blue tapestries was inviting. Yet Julian felt far from comforted. Within those walls was another event filled with watchful eyes, whispered gossip and expectations. Particularly, those of his own mother, Lord and Lady Locshire and Lady Irene.

As he escorted his mother into the large ballroom, which was decorated just as lavishly as Lady Ashvale's had been, if duller in color scheme with simple red and blue hued decorations and flowers, he saw that he had been worse than right. The room was not just filled with nobility. The guest list appeared to be everyone from the most influential and wealthiest families in the ton.

It seemed that Lady Locshire had intended to make an impression by hosting a party for the most prestigious members of high society. That means the gossip will be especially pointed and haughty this evening, Julian thought bitterly, allowing himself a small eye roll while his mother was busy leading the way.

None to his surprise, she guided him toward Lady Irene. Unlike at Lady Ashvale's ball, the young lady was standing alone. And it was clear that she had been searching for them, as well. Or, more specifically, for him.

As they reached her, she curtseyed deeply, although her eyes did not leave his as she did so. Her silver gown shone in the light from the four chandeliers hanging above them with a glare so bright that it could have injured the eyes of a blind man. Julian bowed stiffly, trying to ignore the calculation he saw in Lady Irene's eyes. He glanced at his mother, immediately regretting the decision when he saw the expectant smile on her face.

"Good evening, Lord Rollins," Lady Irene said, cutting off the dowager before she could greet the young lady.

Julian nodded more stiffly than he had bowed.

"Good evening, Lady Irene," he said, fighting against his jaw, which was tightening more with every second that he stood there suffering the woman's coy act.

Augusta stepped up, putting a hand on Lady Irene's shoulder.

"Darling, you look beautiful," she said, giving Julian a pointed glance. "That dress is just perfect."

Lady Irene giggled at the honeyed flattery, and Julian's stomach rolled. He wanted to pretend to have been spotted by someone across the room who wanted his attention. But there were more eyes than those belonging to his mother and Lady Irene on him by then. He swallowed, forcing a tight smile despite the unrest that was sinking in his bowels. It was something that, he realized, had always been there. But after the connection he felt with Miss Hartley that morning, it seemed more blatant and disquieting than ever before.

"Thank you, Lady Rollins," she said, all the while looking right at Julian. Her intentions could not have been clearer. Nor could his mother's. But Julian had no intention of letting on that he understood what was happening in any way. No reaction was best, he felt. Especially since he was determined not to bend on his position regarding Lady Irene.

"Julian, darling, I believe the orchestra will be beginning any moment," the dowager said.

Her message was more pointed than the look in Lady Irene's eyes, which were now fixed firmly on him as though she were trying to will him to read a particular thought. Unfortunately for Julian, he read the thought with perfect clarity. But more unfortunate still, it seemed as though the orchestra conductor read it, as well. For at that moment, the musicians began playing the first lively strains of the first song of the evening. It felt as though the entire room fell silent, waiting for Julian to bend. And at last, he did.

"Lady Irene, would you dance with me?" he asked. He did not try to hide the ice in the offer. Nor did he fail to shoot a hard glance at his mother, who was wearing a most satisfied smile. He also flinched when the young lady took his arm, looking up at him through batting eyelashes.

"I thought you would never ask, Lord Rollins," she said with a playful giggle. Julian thought she sounded like a toddler, which made his skin crawl. She was trying far too hard, and it was more unattractive to him than London's night life. He forced himself to lead her onto the dance floor. But he did not attempt to appear pleased about it. Nor did he bother to smile any longer. Perhaps, he could not make a scene. But no one else could either, just because his expression appeared to be a negative one.

The other dancers watched Julian and Lady Irene as they moved into position. Julian kept more than the proper distance between their bodies, refusing to look at her as they began the dance. They moved through each step of the cotillion in perfect rhythm, both clearly having been well educated in the art of dance. However, Julian's mind and interest could not have been further away from that ballroom. He could not help but notice how shallow and false Lady Irene was. Especially compared to the warmth and sincerity of Miss Hartley. Even he did not dare to admit just why he was so fascinated by her.

The dance blissfully ended, and the announcement that dinner was being served interrupted the dancing portion of the night. Julian would have sighed with relief had he not been required to escort Lady Irene to the dining room. He might have groaned in protest and disgust upon discovering that the pair was seated beside one another, had so many eyes not still been on the two of them. Instead, however, he merely pulled out her chair for her and took his silently, just as the first course of the meal was served.

Conversations buzzed around Julian, but he was as uninterested in them as he was in the lady beside him. Blessedly, his mother was soon engaged by some noblewoman seated beside her, which diverted her attention from Lady Irene and her son. He doubted that would remain the case all evening. However, he would take whatever reprieve he could get.

Lord and Lady Locshire were similarly occupied, the couple laughing along with something that another couple seemed to be animatedly telling them. Julian tried a few sips of the turtle soup in front of him. It was delicious, but the strain of the evening took its toll on his appetite. The only thing for which he hungered was the silence and comfort of his chambers.

Lady Irene, unlike their respective parents, refused to converse with anyone else at the table. She leaned closer to him when the young lady on the other side of her tried to get her attention and lowered her voice.

"Oh, these dinner guests do tire me," she said. Her voice was soft, but Julian did not think it was soft enough to keep the woman from hearing her. "Let us find something interesting to discuss so that we do not have to participate in such drivel."

Julian raised an eyebrow at the young lady. It was not that he did not agree with her. But it was terribly uncouth to speak such thoughts aloud, especially when at such a close social gathering. As Julian suspected, the young lady beside Lady Irene gave her a disgusted look, turning to the person to her left. Julian wanted to smile at the thought that Lady Irene might have alienated herself from a portion of the ton with her careless words. But smiling might have given the young lady the impression that he was interested in what she was saying. He would rather starve to death slowly than to do such a thing, so he kept his expression frozen.

"Your soup is getting cold," he said icily.

Lady Irene glanced down at the bowl and shrugged.

"I do not like turtle soup," she said. "It is too fishy for my taste."

Julian made a sound between a snort and a groan. You will just adore the main course of salmon, then, will you not? He thought with bitter glee.

As he thought, when the main course was finally served, after an eternity of Lady Irene's babble about the inconveniences of social interactions and the life-altering importance of knowing pink from rose shades, the young woman recoiled from her plate. Julian, delighting in the momentary disgust on the distasteful woman's face, took a large bite of the dish, despite his lack of desire to eat. She glanced at him with the first genuine expression he had seen on her face; one of pure horror. Julian savored the bite, pretending not to notice as she scrambled to straighten up her face.

"Well, I must have eaten far too much during the first two courses," she said, returning to her faux sweet, charming persona. "I do not seem to be able to eat one more bite."

Julian nodded.

"Yes, you ate two bites of turtle soup, and one whole roll," he said. "I cannot fathom how satisfied your stomach must be."

Lady Irene looked at him as though trying to determine if he was serious or jesting. Eventually, she laughed, clearly thinking that he was simply trying to be humorous.

"Oh, you are quite funny, Lord Rollins," she said with a high-pitched giggle that gained the attention of the dowager viscountess once more. "I did not know that you enjoyed humor, as well."

Julian tightened his jaw, washing down the unwanted fish with a generous drink of his wine.

"Indeed," he said with all the sarcasm he had been concealing all evening. He was nearing his wits end. Her superficial conversation and deliberate, distasteful flirting were more than Julian could tolerate. If the evening did not end soon, him storming from the dining room would cause the scene he desperately tried to avoid at social events.

Fortunately, dinner concluded with little more than Lady Irene occasionally mentioning the loveliness of the dining room or the clear night sky, which was visible through the window at the far end of the table. Julian could hardly wait to escape to the parlor, where he took up the far back corner, which was quiet and easy to disappear into. Or at least, so he thought.

As he nursed a full glass of brandy, a gentleman approached him. Julian's stomach twisted around the wine and fish he had consumed during dinner when he saw that it was the earl of Locshire.

"Lord Rollins," the man said. His round cheeks were flushed, presumably from his own snifter of brandy, and his gray eyes glittered, as though he had just received the most incredible news.

Julian took another swallow of his brandy, forcing a smile that even to him felt unpleasant and forced.

"Lord Locshire," he said, rising politely from his plush chair to greet the earl. "Please, join me."

He was busy swallowing bile as the earl took him upon his required offer. Julian took his seat again, sitting heavily as his whole body rejected the unwanted company.

The earl, however, looked perfectly pleased with himself. He grinned at Julian, opening his hands as though he were presenting some grand prize.

"I believe this would be a good time to begin discussing the future," he said.

Julian feigned ignorance, raising his eyebrows and opening his eyes innocently.

"I am not sure what you mean," he said.

The earl chuckled.

"Irene said you have quite a sense of humor," he said. "I am talking about future business prospects. You and I can make some excellent partnerships in what I know will be prosperous industries."

Julian shook his head.

"Do you mean that you wish to discuss business?" he asked, trying to ensure that his expression was as serious as he could manage.

The earl laughed again, sipping his brandy and sighing.

"I suppose that in a way, that is what I mean," he said. "We will, after all, have many opportunities to discuss future business ventures. I have a feeling we will be working together very closely. Almost like the son I never had."

The earl was grinning, and Julian's stomach was churning. It was clear to what the earl was hinting. And the longer he spoke, the more Julian wanted to flee the room and never leave his own ever again. But instead, he continued to listen and converse politely, praying silently for the evening to end. Or the world. Whichever came first.

When the torture was at last ended, Julian was too happy to drag his mother to their waiting carriage. He wilted with relief against the bench in the coach, closing his eyes and forcing his shoulder muscles to relax in the hopes of easing the megrim that had settled behind his eyes. However, it seemed that the dowager had no intention of allowing that.

"Julian, I watched Irene and you this evening," she said. "I cannot express how lovely of a young lady she is. She is very accomplished, and she seemed to be having a wonderful time with you. The way she looks at you tells me that she would make the most incredible wife and mother for young Henry and Elizabeth."

Julian's body tensed anew, and he stared at the window. He refused to respond, looking out at the streets they passed and allowing his mother to converse with herself.

"I believe that a union with her is one that would be celebrated throughout the entire ton," she continued as if not noticing that Julian was not engaging with her. You really should consider the future, darling. I do not believe that you could have a better prospect. Such a match would be wonderful for our entire family."

Julian sighed. The dowager was not going to let the issue go. She continued to insist on the match even after he had forbidden her from speaking of him remarrying, and after he had told her that he would never marry Lady Irene. He was as exhausted as he was disgusted, and he shook his head.

"I no longer wish to discuss this matter, Mother," he said. He knew that would not cease the conversation for long. She would likely be right back at it the following day. But for the time being, he would take solace in the tense silence that filled the coach the rest of the trip home. Why did his mother insist on ignoring his demands to drop the marriage topic? What would it take for her to take him seriously?

Chapter Fifteen

"Miss Hartley?" Rebecca asked, making Sophia nearly jump out of her desk. It was one day after receiving her sister's letter, and she had been able to do nothing but worry about her mother. She knew that the money she was making was important for her mother and sister. But that did nothing to quell the overwhelming helplessness she felt. It was like suffocating, despite having plenty of air around her to draw into her lungs. She hated that the redheaded woman had caught her so out of sorts, especially when she was supposed to be focusing on the children's education. But when her family was in such distress, it was all she could do to keep her wits about her.

She rose from her seat, giving the nursemaid a sheepish smile.

"Yes?" she asked, realizing that the children were not with her. "Is everything all right?"

Rebecca smiled softly, nodding as she let the children go into the room.

"The children are taking their time with breakfast this morning," she said. "It would seem that they are using their imagination more lately. Even with their food."

Sophia blushed.

"I apologise," she said. "That must be my fault."

Rebecca shook her head.

"Not at all," she said. "It is wonderful to see them so happy and excited about things again." She paused, studying Sophia. "But you look far less thrilled. I do not believe I have ever seen you so distracted. Is everything well with you?"

Sophia bit her lip. The last thing she wanted was to put her troubles on someone else, especially someone she worked with. But Rebecca felt more like a friend to her with each interaction the two women had. And her kind eyes offered Sophia a genuine invitation to trust someone with her burdens.

"It is my sister," she said. "Well, truthfully, it is my mother.

My sister wrote to me with grave news about her. At least, it sounded grave. I cannot be sure how serious the situation is, as I am not there. Mother had been through a great deal in the past two years, and I know that my absence has not been easy for her. But my sister seems deeply concerned, and I am not sure what to make of it. I only know that I feel terrible for not being there for them when they clearly need me."

Rebecca gave Sophia a sympathetic look.

"I understand just how you feel," she said. "I have worked here for almost three years. When I first left my family, my younger brother fell ill. My father suffered a terrible injury at the factory where he was working until I was sixteen, and it was up to Mother and me to bring in money. So, when I came here, Mother struggled to care for Father and my brother. I worried day and night, wondering if my brother would be all right, if I should quit and return home, if I was doing the right thing by being here."

Sophia's eyes widened.

"Oh, heavens," she breathed, putting her hand over her heart. "Is everything all right? Did your brother survive?"

Rebecca patted Sophia's back and nodded.

"He did," she said. "I took a leave of absence with days I had saved up rather than taking off when they were offered. I helped them for a couple of weeks and took home my pay from the work I performed in the months prior to my return. Gradually, he got better. Father did, as well. With my help and the money I was able to provide, they were able to survive until my brother could go to work. My father eventually took a less strenuous job, and things got back to normal. Now, my money is largely mine, although I still send some home so that my family can afford a few simple luxuries once in a while."

Sophia nodded, wanting to be comforted by the happily ended story. But she had not been there three weeks, let alone three years. She had no rapport with Lord and Lady Rollins, and she certainly did not have any offered days off work to collect.

"I do hope I do not need to return home," she said after thinking over what the nursemaid had said. "But I am worried sick that my family needs me, that they will be upset with me if I do not immediately choose to return home."

Rebecca gave her a kind smile, putting a reassuring arm around her shoulders.

"Do not worry until you have definitive cause to do so," she said. "You will drive yourself mad otherwise. And do not allow yourself to think that your family is upset with you for doing everything you can to help them. I know they understand why you are not there right now. And I have no doubt that they are very proud of you."

Sophia took a deep breath. She knew Rebecca was right. It was not as if she had skipped away from her family to take some arbitrary trip across the country or abandoned them for some quest that would result in disappointment and wasted money or resources. She was absent because she was working, and she was working to help her family.

And of course, her family would be proud of her. They might miss her and wish for her return. But they also understood that not being home was a sacrifice for Sophia, as well. They would never blame her for not being there just because they were having a difficult time adjusting to her absence. And if things got truly bad at home, she would have time to get there and check in, if only for a day or two, and offer the aid she could before she had to return to work. Would she not?

"Thank you, Rebecca," she said, managing to relax a little. She was still worried, but only because she could not help worrying. The nursemaid had offered her much needed reassurance and allowed her to push the darkest of her thoughts and troubled thoughts away. "I cannot thank you enough for your advice and kinship."

Rebecca nodded and smiled, giving Sophia a quick but warm hug.

"Think nothing of it," she said. "I would like to think of us as friends. And I am happy to help in any way I can."

Sophia's smile widened even more.

"I would be honoured for you to call me your friend, Rebecca," she said.

The nursemaid gave her another warm smile.

"I should go and see to it that the children's lunch will be prepared after their morning lessons," she said. "But please, do not hesitate to call me if you should need me."

Sophia nodded.

"Thank you again," she said.

The nursemaid exited the room and Sophia turned to the children.

"All right," she said, allowing the relief from her conversation with her friend to calm her mind. "Shall we begin?"

The children smiled at her and nodded.

"I cannot wait to learn more science," Elizabeth said. "Especially about plants."

Henry nodded again in agreement.

"I love history," he said. "But I also enjoy learning about animals and nature."

Sophia smiled as the children took their seats.

"I enjoy those things, as well," she said. "And I can assure you that there will be plenty more of those lessons to come."

She made her way through their mathematics and penmanship lessons well enough. However, when it came time for their science studies, Sophia's mind began to wander. As she read from their science text, she could not help but think about the times she used to read to Lucy from a similar book. Lucy was curious and eager to learn, much like young Henry. And those thoughts made her more homesick than ever before. Despite Rebecca's words, she could not help worrying about her family. Would they truly be all right? Did they really understand her absence?

Even the children seemed distracted, despite the lesson covering the uses for alchemy in science. After a half hour of unsuccessful attempts to keep the attention of all three of them focused on the book, Sophia finally had an idea.

"Today is such a lovely day," she said. "And I do believe there is more to learn about science outdoors than there is in here. Why do we not take a nature walk around the grounds? We can take sketch books and turn one lesson into both science and art combined."

The children, as she had hoped, instantly brightened. They nodded eagerly, leaving their seats to collect sketch books and some art supplies. Sophia found an old bag behind the bookshelf and helped them load their supplies inside. Then, she led them to the back of the grounds, to the far left path of the gardens. It did not take them long to encounter some bugs which captured the children's attention.

"Why do we not stop here for a moment?" she asked. "I am sure we can find many little creatures and beautiful flowers to draw to spur our creativity. And observing things as they exist in nature can tell us a great deal about the world around us.

The children were digging through the bag before she had even finished speaking. She helped them get started before withdrawing an extra, small sketchbook that she had obtained for herself and a piece of charcoal. The children set out immediately to sketching crickets they saw hopping side by side and pausing to rub together their legs in unison.

Sophia set her gaze on the horizon, admiring the tree line in the distance, as well as a hedge at the halfway mark of the gardens. Two birds sat atop it, singing back and forth to one another. Even from afar, the faint strains of the chirping reached Sophia's ears and the sweet music was a balm to her frantic mind. She began to sketch, keeping one eye on the children as she did so.

Slowly, they moved through the gardens, taking quick notes and making sketches of bugs they saw and particularly beautiful flower blooms. The children teased one another about their drawing abilities, but Sophia could see that it was done with love and jest. It lifted some of the burden from her heart to see them behaving like normal children. She found it easier to relax and take her mind off her own worries as she watched the joy with which they sought satiation to their curiosity.

As they reached a lovely fountain, Sophia saw that the birds she had first spotted were sitting atop it. One of them was splashing in the pool at the top, while the other watched with its head tilted as if wondering what its companion was doing.

"Look at that," Elizabeth said, pointing at the birds. "It is taking a bath."

Sophia nodded, patting the girl on the head.

"That is correct," she said. "Although water does not stick to their wings, birds enjoy playing in water. They do the thorough grooming with their beaks. But nice, cool water feels wonderful to all of us, does it not?"

The children nodded their agreement.

"I see some worms," Henry said, pointing to the ground on the side of the fountain. "May we stay here a bit so that I can draw what they are doing?"

Sophia nodded. She thought she could do with a little more bird watching. And the fountain itself was lovely, with the sound of the gently splashing water coating her raw nerves with its comforting effect. The children chose their spots and set to work, concentrating heavily on their tasks. Sophia stood, holding her book to her chest and admiring the birds a little longer before she resumed her sketching.

She was so focused that she did not hear the approaching footsteps. She was unaware that they were not alone in the garden until she heard the children speak. It was immediately clear to whom they spoke when they summoned Lord Rollins to see what they were doing. She turned slowly in time to meet the viscount's gaze. She took in the coolness of his expression, wondering what he would do. Would he hurry from the gardens and the children who so clearly longed for his approval?

To her surprise, the viscount smiled as he approached the children. He looked tense and nervous, but he also seemed genuinely interested in their work. His face softened as they each explained to him what they were drawing. And her heart stopped when he offered them praise. The way their faces lit up at their father's words warmed her heart. It also made her long for the family she knew she would never get to have. She was usually content with the bond she had built with Henry and Elizabeth. But in moments like those, she desperately wished that she would have children of her own.

When the viscount's eyes met hers once more, her heart began to race. The sheer intensity of his gaze could have melted her where she stood, and shivers raced up and down her spine. His green eyes glimmered with something that, she thought, looked the same way she felt. She did not know what was transpiring between them, but she found it impossible to look away.

Chapter Sixteen

The morning after the ball, Julian dragged himself to join his mother for breakfast in the dining room. He had no appetite as his mind remained occupied by his feelings of unrest. Yet he knew that the dowager would be expecting to converse with him about the previous evening. Specifically, her insistence that Lady Irene was the perfect match for him.

He had once found solace in focusing on his duties as viscount and fulfilling what was expected of him down to the tiniest detail. Now, however, those same things burdened him to his soul. And with the pressure from his mother to remarry, despite his bold attempts to make her drop the subject for good, he felt as though he were attached to anchors and set adrift in the sea, barely able to keep his head above water to keep from drowning.

He was happy to let his mother chatter away about how lovely the ball was and how beautiful Lady Irene was. He let his mind wander, granting the few of his mother's words that he heard noncommittal nods and murmurs of acquiescence. When she excused herself to have tea with Lady Locshire, Julian was too happy to escape the manor himself and lose himself in the gardens.

As he made his way through the shrubs, he told himself that he simply needed some fresh air, that the stuffy event of the previous evening had left him feeling unable to breathe or think, and that he only needed some time in nature. But with each time he peeked around a corner and felt a pang of disappointment, something in the back of his mind reminded him that there was more he sought in the gardens.

He found it as he turned a corner that led to a small stone bench and a large fountain. At the top of the fountain, two red birds flitted back and forth, pecking lightly at the water pooling in the top fountain tier and whistling to one another. But that was not what held Julian's attention. On the other side of the fountain, Henry and Elizabeth sat with what appeared to be books and pencils in their hands, their faces scrunched up in concentration. Behind them, Miss Hartley stood, looking over their shoulders and smiling with warm approval.

He hesitated, not wishing to disrupt yet another of Miss Hartley's lessons. But the part of him that understood he had been hoping to see her and the children in the gardens again was loathe to leave. He watched, intending to stand there only a moment longer before sneaking away and allowing the lesson to finish.

However, before he could do so, Henry and Elizabeth glanced up from their books. Their eyes lit up, and they waved to him, smiling more brightly than Julian had seen in years.

"Papa," Elizabeth said, motioning for him to approach.

"Come see our sketches," Henry said, grinning. "Miss Hartley is allowing us to draw the animals and plants out here in the gardens for our art lesson today."

Ordinarily, Julian would have offered some halfhearted placating response and excused himself to his duties. However, the passion in the voices of his children caught his attention too strongly for him to ignore it. He slowly walked over to where his son sat, pointing at a sketch. There was a bird, which was largely out of frame except for much of its head, beak and one of its feet. On the ground in front of the bird's maw were small, snakelike creatures. Not snakes, he realized quickly. Worms.

Studying the picture as a whole, he also noted a few ants and what appeared to be a caterpillar slinking around the far right edge of the picture. Julian did not realize he was nodding until Henry spoke again.

"Do you like it?" he asked.

Julian met his son's gaze briefly, surprised at the detail in the sketch.

"I do," he said. "Very good, son."

Elizabeth was watching the interaction eagerly. But when Julian made his way to her, she looked down at the ground, blushing. He peeked over her shoulder and saw that she was drawing a bush which had roses on it. He guessed they were white, as the bush seemed to match the bush of white roses that stood directly across from where the children were drawing. But up in the top left corner, as if replacing the sun in her depiction of the landscape around her, there was a lily. He recalled what she had said about her favorite flower, and surmised that in her imagination, it was an orange one.

"That is lovely," he said, surprised at his sincerity. The children were clearly talented with charcoal and paper, and he was amazed at the fervor that was apparent in every line. He found himself smiling just a little as he nodded and looked at Miss Hartley.

The governess was watching him engaging with his children with a flood of warmth. But behind the nurturing compassion, there was something he could not identify. And when their eyes met, he could not identify a single thought at all. It felt as though the whole world melted, leaving only a strong, magnetic bond that stretched between the governess and himself.

It was not the first time he had felt such a connection. But it was more noticeable than the previous times. He wondered if Miss Hartley felt it, too, and the thought was as terrifying as it was intriguing. The longer he stared at her, the harder he found it to look away. Even his thoughts were occupied by her presence and his proximity to her. Why was his heart thumping so fiercely in his chest?

A soft giggle brought him back to the realization of how inappropriate his thoughts were. He cleared his throat, which was already painfully dry and scrambled to regain his senses. He stood up straight enough to feel a few light cracks in his back, setting his face into a more neutral expression.

The children had returned to their sketching, although they would pause occasionally to remark on each other's work or to point out something crawling or flying around them. Julian decided it was the perfect time to ask after the children's progress.

"Is this their art lesson for today, Miss Hartley?" he asked. The words sounded to him like they came across a little harsher than he intended. But the governess simply gave him a small smile and nodded.

"In part, yes," she said. "I thought that since a science text is sometimes difficult to follow without practical knowledge of scientific subjects in real life, it would be a good opportunity to combine an art lesson with science. The children can see how things in nature work in a tangible way, thus making pages in the textbook make more sense when we reach those parts."

Julian nodded, impressed.

"I must say that your eagerness to help the children learn is astounding," he said. "I did not know I could expect such dedication."

The governess blushed, stopping Julian's heart. Was she truly as beautiful as she appeared to him? Or was the sunlight playing tricks on him?

"Your praise is very kind," she said, smiling with sincere modesty and answering his unasked questions. "However, it is their curiosity and their love for learning that inspires me. It is impossible not to want to foster their educational interests. And I have found that it is of the utmost importance to furthering their knowledge to adhere to the lesson methods to which they respond best. It ensures that they retain the lessons and information, and that they understand how to apply and implement them in their lives."

Julian nodded again, finding himself briefly speechless. He had never heard such passion as he did when she spoke about her education methods. He was intrigued by her approach to tutoring his children. He had always been a bit rigid in the routine and structure he expected his children to follow when it came to their lessons. But he realized that with her, she could tell him she was erasing half their current curriculum, and he would not argue.

"Is there anything you can think of that you might need to further these pursuits for their education?" he asked.

Miss Hartley looked surprised for a moment, then smiled again and nodded.

"As a matter of fact, there is something I have been meaning to mention," she said. "I noticed that the schoolroom has not yet been finished. While the nursery serves its purpose, especially since we spend a great deal of time outdoors, I believe that a bit more space for educational tools and books might offer the children more ways to remain passionate about learning. And since

Henry's favorite subject is history and Elizabeth's is botany, I believe that more books on those topics would be dearly appreciated by the children."

Julian nodded. He realized also that he would grant her anything for which she asked. However, in that moment, he told himself that he only meant things she requested or suggested for the children's education. But a voice in the back of his mind whispered to him just how untrue that was.

"Consider it done, Miss Hartley," he said with a small but warm smile. He glanced at the children, who were still alight with the joy their artwork brought them. "And I shall have the room stocked with new art supplies, as well. For them and for you."

The governess's eyes widened, and she stared at him in shock for a moment. The happiness his proclamation had given her was very clear in her eyes, and clearer still in the smile so bright that it rivaled the afternoon sunshine.

"Oh, Lord Rollins, that would be lovely," she said. "I know the children would be most delighted. And it is very kind of you to think of me, as well. They do love when the three of us work on art together. And it is such a joy to comply."

Julian nodded once more. It is quite clear to me that helping my children blossom is a joy to you, my dear, he thought. His cheeks grew hot, and reality hit him like a train. She was, apart from Eliza, the most beautiful woman he had ever seen. And her devotion to his children could never be matched by any woman who was not their mother. But their social stations had not changed. And they never would. Any relationship between a viscount and a governess would be met with disdain and gossip from the ton. He did not need his mother to tell him that that was a gamble he could not make.

"It is no trouble," he said, bowing. "Do forgive my abruptness, but I must tend to some business. I shall make the arrangements to have new books and supplies delivered soon." He reluctantly looked away from the governess to smile tightly at his children. "Continue your hard work, children. Good day to you all."

With that, he turned and headed out of the gardens. He had seen flickers of surprise and hurt in his children's eyes at his sudden departure. But he had seen it in the governess's, as well. If he had believed that any connection he felt with Miss Hartley was in his imagination, the wounded look on her face had clarified that it was not.

And yet, Julian took no pleasure in the fact that he was feeling things he had not believed were possible. He knew what was expected of him, and that nothing could ever be between Miss Hartley and him. But that did not stop him from wishing for something more than the life of responsibilities and noble expectations. The governess reminded him that there were other things to life than duty and conformity. But why should he even entertain such notions when he knew there could never be any such thing for him?

Chapter Seventeen

"I found you, Sister," Henry said as he sneaked up on his little sister.

Sophia watched as Elizabeth squealed with a mix of delight and surprise.

"That is not fair," she said, though she was laughing so hard she could barely breathe. She rose from her hiding place behind a shrub mere paces away from where Sophia sat watching them play, which even the governess had to admit was not a terrific spot to hide. But the girl did not seem upset that her brother had found her so quickly. In fact, she was thrilled to go to the stone bench across from the one on which Sophia sat, ready to count down until she set out to seek her brother.

Two days had passed since she and the children had last encountered the viscount in the gardens. She thought it odd that he kept finding them whenever they left the mansion. Especially since he never came by during lessons to check in on the children's progress. If she did not know better, she might have thought that he was following them. Perhaps he was, and she had not given the notion enough consideration. She shook her head. That was a foolish thought. A viscount surely had better things to do than to secretly stalk his children and the women providing their education. Did he not?

"Sister, you are cheating," Henry said, earning Sophia's attention. But an instant later, he was laughing every bit as hard as his sister, and they went running past Sophia again, shouting unintelligibly in between bouts of giggles. The laughter, combined with the sunlight warming her skin, made her smile. And yet her mind was still haunted by troublesome thoughts about her mother and sister. She had not heard from Lucy since sending her own letter, and for Sophia, that was more worrying than hearing that things had worsened. She hoped that within the next day or so, she would know something more than what she knew right then. And she prayed that it would be good news that reached her.

But her family woes were not the only thing plaguing Sophia. She lay awake each night in the complete silence of a sleeping household, unable to hide from thoughts about Lord Rollins. Each time she saw him, it sparked something in her that she had never before experienced.

She thought he appeared to sense it too, even though he had never said or done anything to confirm her suspicion. She might have thought she was imagining things, if not for the way his smiles changed. At first, they were cold and barely polite. But gradually, they were becoming warm and slow, almost involuntarily and decidedly genuine. And the latter smiles stopped her heart every time.

She would never dare voice any such thoughts. Not even aloud to herself when she was alone. She was well aware that she was a governess, incapable of ever developing such an attachment to any nobleman. She also understood that for the sake of her family's reputation, her decorum had to remain immaculate at all times. It was easy to allow her thoughts to wander at night until she finally drifted off to sleep. But each time she saw the viscount, she longed to have more of a connection with him, despite the impropriety.

"Miss Hartley," Elizabeth said, running up to Sophia gasping for breath. "Come and play with us. Oh, please?"

Sophia laughed again and nodded.

"All right," she said. "Shall I hide, or am I the seeker?"

"Hide," both children yelled in unison as Henry ran up on Sophia and Elizabeth.

Sophia was delighted by how thrilled they were that she agreed to play. She gently ushered them to the statue where they were to hide their faces and count to ten. She waited until both children had their hands securely over their eyes and started preparing to begin counting. Then, she silently tiptoed away backwards, darting around the bushes surrounding the statue and making a sharp turn down another short path nearby.

Just ahead, there was a large hedge that began only two fingers' width from the ground and stopped three heads above hers. She stopped abruptly, just in time to hear the children shout that they were coming for her. She held her breath, trying to suppress laughter as she heard them run in the other direction, calling for her.

She was so focused on listening for their approaching footsteps that she nearly yelped when she stepped on something behind her. When she turned to find that it was a foot, and saw to whom said food was attached, she had to cover her mouth to keep from shrieking. Her heart was racing, but not only because he had startled her. Lord Rollins' stare, which was always so intense and piercing, made every liter of her blood warm.

As it had two days prior when the viscount found them sketching in the gardens, she lost track of her surroundings. It felt as though she were both falling and floating, lost in time and space with nothing but Lord Rollins in existence with her. His penetrating eyes sent a shiver down her spine. The heat in her blood reached her cheeks, setting them on what felt like crimson fire.

Quickly, she looked away, cursing herself for her reaction. She reminded herself of her earlier thoughts, of how improper such feelings for her own noble employer were. She was dangerously close to crossing taboo lines just thinking the things she was in that moment. And yet, despite what she knew about how wrong it was to allow herself such weakness, it was all she could do to not look back up at Lord Rollins once more and throw herself into the deep emerald green pools that were his eyes.

She might have done it, had she not heard Henry's voice just then.

"We found you," he said, tapping her on her shoulder from behind.

"We found you, Miss Hartley," Elizabeth echoed, falling into a fit of giggles.

Sophia turned to face the children, desperately trying to compose herself. But she need not fear her young charges noticing how flustered she was. For her movement exposed their father to the children, and their faces broke into fresh smiles.

"Father, did you come to play with us, as well?" Henry asked.

Lord Rollins glanced at her, almost as if asking for her input. She opened her mouth, unsure of what she would even say. She thought it would be delightful if he played a game with the children. However, despite the way she felt around him and the way he looked at her, he was still her employer. She could never presume to tell him what he should do.

But as she looked into his eyes, she noticed that he appeared to be truly at a loss. He seemed to be struggling with something within, something that was weighing him terribly. Sophia could relate, and she made a rash decision. She gave him an encouraging smile and a quick nod, holding deliberate eye contact as she did so.

After one more second, the viscount smiled and nodded, looking at his children.

"I would be thrilled to join your game," he said.

Sophia's breath caught. He had truly accepted her silent opinion about the children's request. And he had agreed to have the schoolroom finished for them, and to have it filled with new books and supplies. What was happening that he was so willing to consider her advice? Was it possible that there was part of him that was not as cold and unforgiving as people made him out to be, after all?

The children squealed with joy, each of them grabbing one of their father's hands. They led him to the spot where the seeker was to count, explaining to him that it was his turn to hunt for the three of them. He glanced at Sophia, causing her to blush. She offered him another smile before he turned his back to the group. Once he began counting, Sophia hurried off in the opposite direction from whence he had first found her. She tucked herself between two tall rows of hedges that only had the slenderest path running between them. She held her breath, listening. The next sounds delighted her beyond anything she had ever experienced.

The viscount, usually so stoic and not of many words, was making various silly noises with his mouth. It did not take Sophia long to determine that he was trying to get the children to make noise. Nor did it take long for the viscount's tactic to work. Soon enough, she heard muffled snickering from a few hedges ahead of her. It sounded as though Henry had his hand over his mouth, trying his best to stifle laughter and avoid alerting his father to his location.

Just behind Sophia to her left, she heard a full on giggle. Then, a squeal, which told Sophia that Lord Rollins had found his daughter. Or so she thought at first.

"Oh, heavens," she heard him say, his voice echoing loudly through the gardens. "Wherever could my darling Elizabeth be? I cannot find her anywhere."

Another peal of laughter nearly caused Sophia to giggle. She covered her own mouth, listening as footsteps approached her own hiding spot. She froze, waiting to see if the viscount would pass her. And he almost did, until he stopped just in her line of vision and turned around. When he did, her heart stopped once again.

The warmth and joy in his eyes were unlike anything she had ever seen. He looked ten years younger than he was in that moment, the mischief and excitement replacing all the weight and aloof distance she was accustomed to seeing there. A tender, fun viscount had replaced the hard and cold one she had come to know.

She had never thought much about it before, and as the viscount gave her a wink and moved on toward where she thought Henry was hiding, she thought about the pain Lord Rollins must have suffered at losing his wife. Through her observations, it had become clear that he loved her very much. The children clearly had, as well, and her death had seemingly driven a rift between father and daughter and son. And if that was not enough, he had to carry the weight of being a viscount, and he had to do it all alone, without his wife at his side. How heartbreaking, she thought, finally seeing her employer in a different light. *It is no wonder why he is always so standoffish. Would we not all be in his situation?*

She was drawn to him more than she ever had been. And for the time that they played the game, she could pretend that there was no one in the world except for the four of them, and that nothing could cause them pain inside the leafy walls of the gardens.

Disappointment pierced Sophia's beautiful thoughts as a voice rang through the air.

"Julian," the dowager sang, her words echoing through the gardens.

The snorts and giggles died immediately, and no more footsteps sounded around her. There was a pause, and Sophia could almost feel the shift in the atmosphere. Lord Rollins walked past her again, his posture once more rigid and tense, his expression blank and his eyes dead and icy. Sophia's heart ached as the children rushed up behind him.

"Must you go, Papa?" Elizabeth asked, pleading with her father. "Please, stay a little longer."

Lord Rollins shook his head, looking away from his children.

"I must go, Elizabeth," he said. He looked at Sophia, giving her a curt nod. "Good day to you all."

Sophia and the children watched as he marched away from them. It was so evident that he did not want to leave that Sophia considered making up an excuse to call him back to them. If his mother was summoning him, however, she doubted there was anything she could say to make him turn around. So, she, Henry and Elizabeth watched silently as he disappeared from the gardens.

As she stared, she fought with herself. None of what she was thinking or feeling was proper, and she had told herself that many times. However, that did not stop her from thinking and feeling them. In fact, the feelings she had begun developing for him went deeper now than she could ever have anticipated. While she knew that any future with him as anything other than an employer was impossible, she could not help thinking about the connection she knew they shared and the way she was both soothed and unnerved in his presence.

Her heart was burdened as she turned to the children and offered them the brightest smile she could muster.

"Come, children," she said. "Let us go back inside and discuss our drawings."

The children nodded, but all the joy was gone from their expressions. Sophia's heart broke again, desperate to see them smile once again.

"Why do we not find some paints and add some colour to our pictures?" she asked, brightening her voice to sound more cheerful than she felt.

This had some of its intended affect. The children smiled at her, much of the sadness lifting in their faces.

"I love painting," Elizabeth said. "I can make my lily orange, after all."

Sophia nodded, ushering the children in front of her and herding them toward the mansion. She pushed thoughts of Lord Rollins from her mind, reminding herself that her job was too important to her to risk losing over some useless feelings for her employer. Providing for her own family had to be her priority, just as providing a good education for Elizabeth and Henry was. She could not lose focus.

As she got the children back inside and settled with easels and paints, she made a promise to herself. No matter how much she longed for something more, she would not be anything less than professional when it came to Lord Rollins. She would concentrate on being the best governess she could be. Her future, her family's future and the children's future depended on it.

Chapter Eighteen

Julian tried to steady his racing heart as he made his way back to the manor. His feet felt made of cobblestone, making every step away from Miss Hartley more difficult than the previous one. There was no doubt that something had ignited between them as they stood staring at one another during the game of hide-and-seek. It was what he was supposed to make of it and what he should do about it that was the mystery.

He entered the mansion through the open back door, where his mother stood looking at him with an expression that preemptively filled Julian with dread. It was clear there was something on her mind. And he suspected that he knew what it was.

"Darling, we must discuss the picnic tomorrow," she said. "It truly is of the utmost importance, and I want to ensure that everything goes perfectly."

Julian nodded, his mind still lost in the gardens, in that special moment with Miss Hartley. He might have registered that his mother had not mentioned any picnic to him before then, had he not still been so perplexed by the way that the governess both captivated and disconcerted him. But he was, so he followed his mother into the drawing room wordlessly, thinking of nothing but how he wished he had never left the gardens.

"Lord and Lady Locshire spoke at length about the picnic at the ball," Augusta said before they had even taken their seats. "I believe that this outing will be the perfect chance for you to spend some time with Irene."

Julian nodded vaguely, his thoughts slowly turning. She certainly wastes no time, he thought, suppressing a sneer.

"I knew nothing of this picnic," he said as the fog of enchantment in his mind gave way to bitterness and disgust. There would never be any chance that he would be interested in Lady Irene. No matter how much effort his mother put into placing her in his path.

The dowager shrugged.

"I cannot overstate the cruciality of your role in securing the future for us," she said. "And the future of your children, as well. Julian, society has certain expectations, and you must keep those in mind with everything you do."

Julian listened, grinding his teeth back and forth as he chewed on the words he wished to say. He was tired of having the same discussion with his mother. Perhaps, if he simply sat in silence, she would dismiss him and end the conversation. If only for the moment.

"Julian, darling," she said again. "You truly must consider a union with Irene. She is an excellent match, and as I have told you before, she is interested in a marriage to you."

"I will never consider rushing into a loveless marriage," he snapped, unable to keep his thoughts to himself any longer. "I do not expect to make you understand. I only expect that you will respect my decision and make no further attempts to force me into something that I have no intention of doing."

The dowager sighed, shaking her head.

"I do not think that you understand the importance of good marriages in the ton," she said. "Especially when you have children without a mother."

Julian glared at his mother, copying her head shake.

"I do not think you understand what a loveless marriage would do to the children," he said. "Or to me, for that matter. A home that feels largely hollow and superficial is sure to do more damage than one with only a father. And I refuse to live such a life, Mother. How many times must I explain that to you?"

Augusta gave her son a pitying smile; one which infuriated and embarrassed Julian, despite having not done anything humiliating.

"Having children means that you must do everything that is in their best interest, Julian," she said. "Even if they do not like it. And even if you do not, either. You have duties to me, as well, as I have tirelessly mentioned. Your viscount responsibilities and your family are more important than what you want. You must keep your priorities in order."

Julian sighed. Even if his mother were not entirely wrong, and even if some of her intentions incidentally happened to be pure and focused on the children's and his best interest, he could not simply toss himself at someone like Lady Irene. And yet, he could not deny the truth in some of her words. With his increasingly frequent encounters with the governess and the children, it was becoming ever clearer that Henry and Elizabeth needed a maternal figure in their lives. That was one thing he could not deny. And if he had his way, it would be a woman like Miss Hartley.

And yet, that was the very thing giving him such trouble. When he allowed his thoughts about the governess to wander, he could imagine a world in which the children could have a mother like her. He would allow himself to admit that he could see an almost identical compassion, love and concern for the children, and a fearlessness when speaking with him that he had seen in Eliza.

He also imagined that the spark he felt any time he was near her could help them build a beautiful life, caring for the children without any concern for what society thought of the matter. There was an undeniable attraction for her, and in those thoughts, he could not deny it. Different social statuses notwithstanding, he felt something about her that he had not felt, or believed he ever could feel, after losing Eliza.

How can I comply with Mother and still have a real, true connection? He wondered as his mother watched him, waiting for him to respond. He was torn between two impossibilities, and he did not see any way that one of them could be circumvented. But nor did he see any way that his mother would ever drop the subject. And no amount of him rejecting her pressure or telling her to stop speaking about it would change it.

On his way to his chambers, he passed by the schoolroom. That sparked the memory of his promise to Miss Hartley. He rushed back downstairs, seeking out Mrs. Barnes. He found her speaking with a maid about duties. When the housekeeper spotted him, however, she dismissed the woman and curtseyed.

"Good day, milord," she said warmly.

Julian gave her a nod.

"I need the staff to see to it that the schoolroom is finished as quickly as possible," he said. "I would also like for more history and botany books to be purchased, as well as all the kinds of paint supplies there are." He paused, recalling one more thing. "And get some new books by Jane Austen, as well as some more works of Shakespeare. Any that we do not already have in the library are acceptable."

Mrs. Barnes beamed at him and nodded.

"Right away, milord," she said. "Do you have any special instructions for the schoolroom?"

Julian started to shake his head. Then, another thought struck him, and he smiled.

"Have orange lilies, gardenias and pink roses painted on the walls, as well as placed in separate vases all throughout the room."

The housekeeper looked briefly surprised, but she quickly nodded.

"As you wish, Lord Rollins," she said.

***

Julian forgot that they were expecting company until he entered the dining room. But when he saw the guests, his heart lifted.

"George and Susan," he said, approaching his brother and sister-in-law. "Forgive my vague forgetfulness. It must have slipped my mind that the two of you were coming. I am delighted to see you."

George rose, clapping his brother on the back.

"It is good to know that we are so important to you, Brother," he said, playfully nudging Julian's shoulder with his fist.

Julian rolled his eyes as he kissed Susan on the cheek.

"If your husband winds up missing, I promise I know precisely where he is," he said with a chuckle.

Susan giggled, returning Julian's kiss.

"I can always help distract the authorities," she said.

The brothers laughed as everyone took their seats again.

Even the dowager seemed relaxed and eager to enjoy a nice family meal. Julian also allowed himself to be at ease. It was always a wonderful time when George and Susan came to visit. He believed that the dinner would be just what he needed to escape all the strain and conflict he had experienced of late.

"I can hardly believe that Susan and I have been married for six months," George said after the main course was served.

Susan beamed at her husband, blushing and nodding.

"It feels like it's been less than six days," she said. "I never had any doubts about marrying you. But it is as if our marriage gets better every day."

Augusta smiled knowingly at her youngest son.

"Marriage is one of the most wonderful experiences one can have," she said. "I daresay that it is second only to having children, which is an unrivaled blessing."

Julian nodded in agreement. He had been neglectful of his children after Eliza passed. But the precious moments, like earlier that day when he played hide-and-seek with them, reminded him just how much he adored his children. Even though he never even got to hold his third child, he loved that one, as well. And for all the heartache he had experienced, he would not have traded fatherhood for anything.

Susan nodded eagerly.

"We are thrilled to start a family," she said, her face glowing. "We have already picked out names for two boys and two girls."

Augusta's face lit up. One thing for which Julian had to give his mother credit was that she had always enjoyed her role as a grandmother. Even though she was a detached mother, especially since his father died, he never doubted her love for his children. And he had no doubt that she would love George's and Susan's future children every bit as much.

"Oh, what are they?" she asked with a dreamy expression on her face.

As everyone continued talking, Julian slipped into his thoughts. A sudden pang of wistfulness struck him, and he realized just how deep his own emptiness truly went. He never forgot how much he had loved Eliza. But in his quest to keep her memory alive, he had forgotten how much companionship and a sense of family had meant to him.

After dinner, George joined Julian in the parlor, while their mother and Susan adjourned to the drawing room. Julian poured them some brandy, which they sipped in silence for a moment. Julian's thoughts were just beginning to drift back to his feelings at dinner, as well as the conflicting ones he felt for Miss Hartley, when George spoke.

"Julian," he said. "I have been looking for the chance to ask you how you are doing." He paused, holding up a finger. "And I mean truly. You need not give me plastic platitudes and vague assurances. I am your brother, and I care about your welfare and contentment."

Julian opened his mouth to plead ignorance until he could find a satisfactory answer. But George was giving him a look that told him he would not succeed. George had always been highly intuitive. If he had not noticed Julian's wandering mind at dinner, he surely had at recent social events. Or he had noticed the lack of Julian's presence at White's, or even at the townhouse that George shared with his wife. Whatever the case, nonsense from Julian would not be acceptable.

"I admit that I have something of an issue," he said with a sigh. "It is my new governess. I seem to find myself attracted to her. Incredibly so, if I am to be honest. She is not only wonderful with the children, but she is also kind, warm and compassionate. And she does not flinch around me as so many other people do. I find that I think about her constantly and that I never want to leave my encounters with her."

George was nodding well after Julian fell silent. After it became clear that Julian was waiting for a reply, George shrugged.

"I am merely waiting to hear the part that is the trouble," he said.

Julian stared at his brother, waiting for the punchline to a joke. When it did not come, he raised his eyebrows.

"Besides the fact that I am a viscount, and she is a governess?" he asked, bewildered. "I suppose nothing at all."

George chuckled.

"I am aware that the two of you are of different stations," he said. "I am just unsure as to why that matters when she makes you feel the way you have described to me."

Julian opened his mouth to recite the rhetoric that their mother would have delivered without a thought. But he closed his mouth, thinking about what his brother said. If it were not for what society thought, what would Julian himself think about it?

"Mother has been pressing for me to marry Lady Irene, as you well know," he said. "I could only guess what her reaction would be if I told her that I had taken an interest in a governess."

George laughed again, taking another sip of his drink.

"As can I, Brother," he said with a shake of his head. "And yet again, I say that I cannot think of a reason why you should let that get in your way."

The return to the question made Julian fall silent. It seemed so simple when George said the words. But was it really as easy as doing what he wanted, despite what was demanded of him and his station?

"Julian, you must think of your own happiness," George continued. "Society has rules and laws that protect us and keep us safe. And then, it has expectations and beliefs that do nothing apart from dictate the lives of others, based on what some people think should be or should occur. But where will society be when we are on our deathbeds and seeking comfort? Where will society be when we are in our darkest moments? Finding something, or someone, who makes you genuinely happy is nearly impossible, as I know you are aware. You should never let someone else tell you what that should be." He paused with a knowing smirk. "Or who."

Julian sighed.

"Even if you are right, how could I ever make such a thing happen?" he asked.

George gave him a slow nod.

"I believe that you already know," he said.

Soon after, George and Susan bade farewell to Augusta and Julian. The exhausted viscount went to his chambers, still thinking of the governess, and of what his brother had said to him. He could never allow himself to settle for some barely mediocre existence, no matter who believed that he should. But finding a way to have both what he wanted and needed would be far from easy.

As he sat on the edge of his bed, dreading the picnic the following day, he realized that he had to find some way. He had had love once. And for the first time since, he was beginning to believe that he could again. It might be difficult, and it might make for a strange path ahead of him. But he was beginning to realize that he wanted the happiness of which George spoke. And he did not think he could give up an opportunity to have it, not when it felt so close.

Chapter Nineteen

The only moments of peace that Julian could boast the following day were those spent as Alexander helped him dress for the picnic. The moment he set foot out of his room, the hectic preparations were evident. He thought to sneak away and spend every single moment possible away from the flurry of servants and the orders being issued by his mother that seemed to ring out from every hallway. But as he slunk toward the library, his mother, appearing out of nowhere, stopped him.

"I trust you are prepared to take up your mantle of welcoming the guests," she said. "They will be arriving at any moment."

Julian looked at her, wanting to point out that she had been the one to organize the event, and that its only purpose was to pressure him into matching with Lady Irene, despite the numerous times he had protested. But upsetting his mother right then would only leave him responsible for hosting the picnic, and he was of no mind to do so.

"Yes, Mother," he sighed, not bothering to hide his distaste and disappointment.

The dowager chose to ignore her son's feelings. She gave him a sweet smile and nodded.

"Good," she said. "I shall go ensure that the food has been prepared and that the maids are taking it from the kitchens to the clearing now."

Julian did not nod, and his mother did not wait for him to do so. She hurried off, leaving him to turn and head the opposite direction, toward the front door of the manor. He thought the guests might still be an hour or so from arriving, based on the activity still filling the manor in preparation for them. But he dutifully took his place at the end of the foyer, as ready as he would ever be to greet the people that would soon fill the back grounds of Rollins Manor.

As he greeted each guest, the chaos in his mind raged. Every smile and polite greeting felt like a rope around his throat, tightening and choking him with unverbalised expectations and judgments. He understood it would be a trying day. He just hoped to find some way to pass the hours so that he could be alone with his thoughts again.

The last of the guests to arrive were Lord and Lady Locshire and Lady Irene. He greeted them, his entire being tensing at the sight of the woman his mother so desperately wished for him to marry. He did not need to look at Lady Irene's parents to know what they felt he should do. He offered her his arm after responding to their greetings with a deep bow, giving her a mechanical smile.

"Allow me to escort you to the clearing," he said, his voice sounding as artificially engineered as his expression felt.

Lady Irene did not notice. Or at least, she pretended not to. She took his arm, managing a modest blush as she smiled up at him.

"I would be delighted," she said. "It was lovely of Lady Rollins to organise such a lovely picnic."

Julian just managed not to roll his eyes. You have not even seen the picnic to know whether it was lovely, he thought, biting his cheek to keep from speaking the words aloud.

"It was certainly unexpected," he said, offering nothing more in the way of conversation as he led Lady Irene and her parents through the gardens and to the clearing, where the other guests mingled. From around the corner, he could see gold and silver decorated white, black, and brown carriages littering the grounds of his family estate. Julian closed his eyes as though he could magically wish them all away. He was unsurprised when he opened them again and saw all the coaches still right where his restless vision had left them. He wondered how his mother could have arranged such a large event without him noticing. But he thought again about how preoccupied he had been and realized that he would not have paid any heed even if she had told him well in advance.

Upon seeing Lady Irene, a group of young ladies approached, gushing over her arrival.

"It is wonderful to see you, Irene," one of them said, throwing her arms around the young woman.

Lady Irene beamed at the group, greeting all four of them in turn.

"It is lovely to see you all here, as well," she said.

Another young woman in a pink dress stepped forward, linking her arm through that of Lady Irene.

"Will you come join us for the picnic?" she asked.

Julian's hopes rose. Perhaps Lady Irene would find herself preoccupied with friends and too busy to attach herself to him. But this thought was crushed as Lady Irene pretended not to glance at him over her shoulder in such a way that the other ladies just happened to notice.

"I am afraid that I have already promised my company to someone else," she said too sweetly.

The women looked past her at Julian, who made himself appear interested in looking around the rapidly filling grounds of Rollins Manor. Speaking with Lady Irene was bad enough, in his opinion. He would not get caught up in conversing with four more women who were clearly just like her.

The first woman spoke again, giving Lady Irene a knowing look.

"Of course, darling," she said. "I do hope that you will join us for a game or two later." She, too, glanced at Julian as she spoke, but the viscount held fast to his mission of ignoring anything the women said. And eventually, they departed, leaving him alone with Lady Irene.

"They are such dear friends," she said. "Perhaps I will sit and visit with them a bit later. I would not want to miss the opportunity to sit with you while we enjoy our meal."

Julian sniffed, masking his bitter disappointment with a tight smile.

"That would be a terrible shame," he said.

Lady Irene giggled, the sound grating Julian's nerves raw. The sound was faker each time he heard it, and he did not know how many more times he could hear it.

"I just adore your sense of humor," she said in her too sweet tone.

Julian desperately wanted to correct her and let her know that he never joked, at least not with her. But he thought again about the repercussions of creating a scene, and just barely managed to keep his mouth shut.

To his relief, ten minutes later, Lady Irene's friends called to her from across the back grounds. They were preparing to play badminton and they wanted her to join one of their pairs. She looked at him and, for a moment, Julian saw a glimpse of the true boredom and the relief at the chance to get away from him that she felt before she gave him that honey smile once more.

"I do hope you do not mind," she said. "Badminton is my favourite game."

Julian hid his own relief by bowing.

"Not at all," he said. "You may go."

Lady Irene batted her eyelashes at him over her shoulder long enough that he grew tired of it and turned his back on her. When he heard the game was to begin, he turned back around. He could see the temporary badminton court from his position, and he watched Lady Irene take her place. He was hardly surprised when, within the first full minute of the game, he observed how bad she was at the game, disproving her love for it. With a smug smirk and a shake of his head, he glanced around looking for his mother. And when he did not see her, he slipped away from the group and darted around some bushes.

He had no destination in mind as he moved further and further away from the picnic. As the voices grew fainter, the calm that fell over him grew greater. He allowed himself the chance to forget that behind him was a large group of people he was hosting at his home against his will. He tilted back his head, listening to birds singing in the distance and watching white clouds roll slowly in the sky above his head.

He recognized the voice he heard as soon as it reached his ears. Miss Hartley was saying something. And based on the proximity, she sounded very close. He kept walking toward the sound until he spotted the children and her beneath a large tree. He slowly approached, not wanting to startle anyone. But when he heard what she was saying, he stopped, enraptured.

"The little housekeeper did not know what she should do," she said. "Her employer was sad, and she wished to help him to feel better. She knew she loved him, even though he was a wealthy duke. But all she cared about was doing something that would make him happy again. Even if that was not what other people believed that she should do."

Julian's heart thudded in his chest as George's words once more raced through his head. Society will not be with you in your darkest moments...

No, he thought as the governess's musical voice gave him chills. But the people who love you well, the people you love well, will be there always.

As he watched Miss Hartley weave the story she was apparently telling, he watched the delight on his children's face. They were lost in her words, their expressions showing him how much they enjoyed storytelling.

"And then, the duke asked the housekeeper to marry him," Miss Hartley said as he took a step closer. "The end."

The children clapped wildly, giving small shouts of excitement.

"Could that truly happen, Miss Hartley?" Elizabeth asked.

Henry waved his hand, although he was too excited to wait until called upon to speak.

"I know that if I were a duke, I would marry whoever I loved," he said. "It would not matter what they were."

The governess gave the children a tender smile.

"It is whomever, Henry," she said with the gentlest encouragement. "And I believe that if we want something badly enough, no matter how impossible it might seem, we can make it happen."

Elizabeth was pacified with her answer, and Henry was smiling fondly at the governess. Julian was enthralled with the young governess. And suddenly, he could not stand back and watch the three of them from afar any longer.

"Has anyone heard the story about the prince who had to rescue the princess he loved?" he asked, giving his voice a dramatic, exaggerated flair, as though he were an actor on a stage.

Everyone looked up at him, surprised by his arrival. He gave Miss Hartley, who stood speechless, a waggle of his eyebrow, then turned his attention back to his children.

Elizabeth laughed.

"Oh, Father, there are lots of stories like that," she said.

Julian shook his head, putting his fists on his hips in a playfully offended manner.

"Not like this one," he said. "If you will all be so kind, I shall regale you with this special tale."

Henry and Elizabeth exchanged dubious glances, but they were smiling and motioning for their father to join them. Julian gave the governess another glance and saw that she was hiding a smile behind her hand. He could not help smiling himself as he took her spot in front of the children. He paused to take a stance that was as dramatic as his entrance to the storytelling circle and waited for the children and Miss Hartley to get comfortable once more. Then, he cleared his throat loudly.

"This is a tale about a prince who met a princess who was out on a grand quest," he said. "The quest was that she wished to spread the wonders of magic all throughout the land. But her parents died before they could assign a knight to complete the mission for her. Thus, unable to claim the throne for herself and appoint a hero, and unwilling to send some knight to what would surely be his death, she decided that she would fulfill the quest herself."

Julian looked at the governess, pleased to discover that he had her complete attention. *Good*, he thought. *She and her passion for educating are my inspiration for this tale, after all.* That was a thought that he would never speak aloud. However, it was completely true. And with his muse in mind, he began his tale.

"Once upon a time, there was a hermit prince," he said. "This prince ruled over a large kingdom but was rarely seen outside his palace walls. But one day, he was riding to a neighbouring village and met the most beautiful woman he had ever seen. She was dressed in a simple gray dress, with her torso, arms and legs wrapped in pieces of tough leather. Little did he know that she was a princess."

He carried on with his tale, pulling line after line as if he had written it prior to his performance. Both his children and Miss Hartley were utterly enraptured, and he relished the awe and wonder on all three of their faces. It was the first time the children had looked at him that way since he used to read to them when they were little. And it was the first time that the governess had ever looked at him like that. He felt as though he was on top of the world.

But even as he reveled in the joy of the moment, dread bubbled just beneath the delight of his storytelling. No matter how wonderful of a time he was having, it could not last forever. Eventually, his tranquility would be broken and he would be forced to return to the world of snobby nobility and stuffy conversations. The comfort that Miss Hartley's presence brought him would dissolve, replaced by the desire to flee the country anytime Lady Irene was nearby. He knew that no matter how much his soul cried to remain in the security of the feelings he was currently experiencing, he would soon have to return to the picnic. And the realization was almost too much to bear.

Chapter Twenty

Sophia stared, mesmerized, as Lord Rollins told his imaginative tale. She noticed how enthralled the children were with his every word, and it did not take long for her to become just as spellbound. She had not had many chances to hear him speak before that day, and none that were more than brief and cursory and interrupted by his responsibilities calling him away from her and the children. But that day, she realized how melodious and magnificent his voice was. He projected it so that it rang clearly through the air, each word another brushstroke to the painting that was the verbal literature he was creating with his storytelling.

She could clearly picture each geographical land piece he described and imagine herself in the adventures he was detailing. The fiction crafting alone was worthy of praise. But that was not what held the majority of Sophia's attention.

Right before her eyes, she witnessed her employer step outside his usual conservative, cool attitude, losing himself in something as simplistically delightful as the art of telling a well thought out tale. But there was more still than that. He was evidently reveling in the joy it brought to his children, his eyes twinkling each time one of them gasped or giggled with glee. It was something Sophia believed she would never witness.

"Oh, Papa," Elizabeth said with eager excitement. "Do tell me that the prince gets to hold the princess's hand. Please?"

Sophia giggled at the little girl's invested interest in the story. She glanced at the viscount to witness his reaction, only to find that his gaze was fixed on her. Her heart skipped and she felt her cheeks grow hot. But she could not bring herself to look away until Lord Rollins slowly redirected his attention to his daughter.

"In due time, dear Elizabeth," he said, his voice still thick with the dramatic flair with which he was telling his story. "He must get through his sea voyage and find the giants which hold her captive."

As he spoke the last words, he glanced at Sophia again. The

intensity in his eyes made her heart flutter once more, and she had to concentrate to catch her breath. It was not impossible to imagine, if only for a moment, that he was the prince in his tale, and that he wove his tale with a special princess in mind. And with the look in his eyes as she smiled at him, it was just as easy to think that the princess could be her.

Whatever the truth behind his story, Sophia found it impossible to resist the allure of the magical resonance of the moment. Her emotions spilled over with wishful approbation. He spoke of a sea disrupted by impossible storms and sea creatures, but his eyes spoke of an experience that made him feel as though he had truly lived through such trials. And he told the story with such fervor that Sophia saw more than a nobleman for whom she worked, who was no more an acquaintance to her than a beggar on the street.

She could see the man behind the walls which kept him guarded and the burdens of his role as viscount. She saw Lord Julian Rollins, not his responsibilities and duties. It seemed that he felt more comfortable, as well, as though he was truly getting to be the version of himself that made him feel something other than professional detachment toward everything in his life. But most importantly, she could see that the children noticed the change in their father. They were warming up to him faster with each passing day, with each surprise interaction they had with their father. It offered her soul great comfort, as though she was getting to witness Lord Rollins open up his heart to his children for the very first time. She had never doubted his love for them. But she sometimes thought they did. And seeing that doubt slowly dissolve within them was touching and heartening.

"At last, the prince found the caves where the giants were said to be hiding," he said. "They were hidden by the trunks of the largest, tallest trees that the prince had ever seen. It took him three whole days and three whole nights to walk around the base of the tree that housed the first of the giants."

Henry's eyes grew wide, and he leaned forward.

"Heavens," he said. "What did he do for food and water? You said he ran out of supplies right before he reached the forest where the giants were."

Sophia watched, hiding her amusement by biting her lip and glancing away for the briefest of seconds. The viscount did not look bothered by the impossibility of this portion of his tale, however. Rather, he grinned at his son, giving Sophia a wink so small that she was uncertain as to whether she truly saw it.

"There were small animals that burrowed down into the roots of the trees," he said. "He hunted them on his journey around the trees during the day and lit fires to cook them at night. And the trees had leaves so large that they held water like bowls. Once he realized this, he simply fashioned a spear out of a stick and part of a broken blade and poked holes in leaves above his head until he felt water dripping on his head. He filled up his sheep's skin and continued on his way."

The children murmured, accepting his explanation as plausible. Julian continued the tale, and Sophia listened as he described the battle with the first giant. Once again, he looked up at her, and she could picture the event as though she were truly living it. The bond she was sure was being built between them was stronger than ever, and she knew that he had to feel it, as well. For just a moment, she allowed herself to imagine that they lived in a world where they could express a true, sweet, genuine love for one another and build a life together with the two most wonderful children in all of England. She pictured herself having children of her own, with him, and of them living the rest of their lives happy and free of any stigma or shunning that would, in reality, result from a union between the two of them.

"Can you tell us how the prince plans to defeat the rest of the giants once he reaches them?" she asked, surprising even herself by speaking.

She feared that Lord Rollins would be irritated by her interruption. Instead, however, he gave her a smile that, had she not known better, she could have sworn held a special secret behind it. He stared at her for just a second longer than was necessary before pretending to go into deep thought.

"He has been plotting this confrontation for some time now," he said, once more giving her an intense stare. "And while he is unsure of exactly what his plan might be, he will let the situation and circumstances be his guides. For you see, it is not the giants which are the most important part of his journey. It is getting to be with his princess once the giants have been neutralised."

Sophia's heart fluttered, and although she blinked rapidly at the incredible sensation, she was sure she saw him wink and give her a crooked, slow smirk. Could he truly be talking about her as the princess, as she had allowed herself to imagine?

"I bet he uses an enchanted sword," Henry said, jumping to his feet and swinging an imaginary blade.

Elizabeth shook her head furiously.

"He does not have an enchanted sword, silly," she said. "He will have to use a giant's club."

Henry looked at his sister with horrified eyes.

"A giant's club will be too heavy for him," he said.

Elizabeth stuck out her tongue at her brother.

"Not if the princess uses her magic to help him," she said.

Sophia bit her lip to stifle her laughter. The gentle banter between the siblings was so refreshing, but she needed to intervene.

"Children, settle," she said. "Let your father finish the story so that we may find out how the prince defeats the giants."

The children glanced at each other and nodded.

"Yes, of course, "Elizabeth said, sounding very grown-up. "Please continue, Father."

The viscount gave Sophia another look, this one of astonishment and gratitude. Then, he continued his tale, and Sophia was once again lost in the imaginary world of magic and impossible obstacles.

But as with all good things, the viscount's story eventually came to an end. Sophia and the children all rose and applauded, and Sophia watched giddily as the nobleman gave them exaggerated bows and bellows of gratitude. He was an excellent showman, and Sophia thought again about how youthful and burden-free he appeared. She knew she was seeing the real Lord Julian Rollins right then. She also knew that she would do anything to keep that man around a while longer. She told herself the wish was for the children. But deep down, she did not want to let him go, either.

However, as the applause died and the children quieted, Lord Rollins' expression changed once more. Gone was the carefree sparkle in his green eyes, the rosiness in his cheeks and the relaxed, boyish smile. The cold gloss returned to his stare, his face went pale, and his mouth was drooping into what she knew would be a thin pressed line within minutes.

"This has been wonderful," he said, sadness flickering in his cool eyes. "However, I must return to the picnic. Mother will surely be looking for me soon, and I would not wish to have her disturb your afternoon."

The children's happy expressions also transformed. They ran to their father, their eyes wide and pleading, and Elizabeth's filled with tears.

"Oh, Papa, please do not go," she said, squeezing him as tightly as she could with her little arms.

Henry nodded, gripping onto his father's coat sleeve.

"Let us tell you a story now, Father," he said. "You could tell Grandmother that we needed your help with a lesson."

To Sophia's surprise, the viscount paused, and she could see that he was clearly contemplating the idea. She held her breath, wondering if he would truly shirk the event and spend the rest of the afternoon with his children. But as if reality hit them both in the head like a ball of hail, he shook his head, the remorse deepening in his eyes.

"I am truly sorry, children," he said. "I must be going. Behave for Miss Hartley. I shall see all of you another time. Good day, everyone."

On his last word, he looked at Sophia once more, and her heart ached. The reluctance screamed for her to rescue him from this duty, but she knew there was nothing she could do but watch helplessly. And as he departed, she found that she, too, had tears stinging her eyes. She blinked them furiously away, pushing aside all her selfish thoughts. Her concern was for the two terribly disappointed children, who she knew would be difficult to console.

"Why do we not go inside and have a little tea party?" she asked, determined to cherish the wonderful moments they had gotten to share with the viscount. "We can ask the cook to make any treats you wish."

The children nodded, but their smiles were smaller and less prominent. Sophia's heart felt bruised. Why did society have to make it so difficult for a father to enjoy the simplest of pleasures with his children?

Chapter Twenty-one

"Can we read that part of the story once more?" Elizabeth asked as Sophia prepared to turn the page of the book she was reading. She had chosen Pride and Prejudice by Jane Austen after much insistence from the children. During the three days since they had all witnessed the incredible yarn spinning of the viscount, all the children wanted to discuss was fictional literature and storytelling.

Sophia laughed, nodding as she flipped back to the beginning of the chapter.

"Very well," she said. "But do not forget, this is a reading assignment. I will need you to pay close attention to the details, as you will need to answer questions regarding the story once we have finished the book."

The children nodded, although Sophia was sure they barely heard what she said. That was perfectly all right with her, as the children had never been happier than they had been over the past few days, and certainly not as joyful as they had been that morning. The new schoolroom had been more than she could have hoped for, complete with paintings of all their favorite flowers all over the walls.

It seemed as though the children were especially inspired by the bright colors, polished bookshelves that were filled to bursting with books on their favorite subjects and the art corner, which was set up and ready anytime they wished to start painting. Even their arithmetic lesson had gone flawlessly, with the children making up their own games at their seats when the time had come to solve the problems on the blackboard.

As the little girl requested, she began rereading the tenth chapter of the book again. Her eyes lit up with each page Sophia turned, and Henry mouthed words he remembered from the first two times Sophia had read the chapter, looking as animated as his father had when he was telling his story in the gardens three days prior. He reminded Sophia so much of Lord Rollins in that moment that her thoughts slipped back to her employer, despite reveling in the delight that came with educating her precious charges.

She had spent countless hours trying to convince herself that the special moments she felt she shared with the viscount were as fictional as the story he told the children and her. But her dreams of late painted a different picture. In them, Lord Rollins was weaving another tale, one in which a viscount and a governess found true love and married, living as happily as the princesses in children's storybooks.

They danced at grand balls, proclaiming their love to the world with each step as they twirled amidst admiring onlookers. She always awoke with her heart racing and longing to see Lord Rollins' face. And reality always seemed foggy and uncertain as she pulled herself from the fantasy.

But as she watched young Henry mimic his father's gestures and facial expressions, reality became clear once more. Her dreams would never be anything more, as her station in life was too far below his to ever allow for such a romance. He was a prince, if not a king, in her eyes. But she would never be anything close to a princess. And royalty never fell in love with peasants. Not in reality, to be certain.

Once she finished the chapter for the third time, she closed the book, setting it aside. She smiled at the children, who stared dreamily in the direction of the desk drawer, where the novel now rested. She allowed the two of them to wander in their thoughts for a moment, watching their eyes dance as their imaginations played out performances of what she had just read to them based on their understanding of the story. It was so quiet for a minute that when Elizabeth spoke, it nearly startled her.

"Miss Hartley," she said sweetly and with more confidence than the timid little seven-year-old girl who Sophia had first met. "May we go into the gardens and gather some flowers? Please?"

Henry nodded his agreement with his sister.

"We need some fresh ones for our bedsides," he said. "And perhaps you could collect some for yours, as well."

Sophia smiled. She hardly needed convincing for the opportunity to gather flowers. And while she realized that they might well run into the viscount again, she also knew it was worth taking the chance. Besides, the more excited the children got about their education and about exploring the world around them, the more they blossomed into happy, outgoing children. And that was a transformation that soothed her heart in ways that nothing else could.

"Please, Miss Hartley?" Elizabeth asked, batting her eyelashes at her governess as though afraid she had not made a strong enough of a plea the first time.

Sophia giggled. She gave them a slow, exaggerated sigh as though the task were a large chore. But she winked at them, nodding as she gestured toward the door.

"I suppose we could go out for a little while," she said, speaking slowly and deliberately to drag out embarking on the excursion just a little longer.

The children were ahead of her, however. They were halfway down the stairs before Sophia reached the top of the staircase. They waited eagerly for her by the back door, opening it and rushing outside as soon as they could see her approaching. She followed them out, directly to the heart of the gardens, where some of the prettiest roses grew. The sun felt like warm hands caressing Sophia's cheeks, and she took in deep breaths of the fresh, sweet-smelling air. Elizabeth began carefully plucking some white roses, while Henry went straight for the yellow ones.

Following suit, she walked to a red rose bush. She knew that Henry would wish to have some gardenias, and Elizabeth would be begging for orange lilies. She intended for their little group to slowly make their way from those rose bushes and the surrounding hedges to the bushes where their respective favorite flowers grew. But as they were making their second turn heading toward the lilies, a shadow crossed their path. Sophia did not need to look up to see who had intercepted them once more.

"Papa," Elizabeth said, rushing up to her father with her flowers in her hand.

When she did look up, she saw that Lord Rollins was dressed in hunter green riding attire and that there was a line of sweat running across his forehead. It appeared that he had just finished a morning horseback ride. He did not notice them until the children called out to him.

"Papa," Elizabeth said, breaking away from Sophia and running toward the viscount.

Henry chased after his sister, holding his fistful of flowers in his hand.

"Father," he said, reaching their father at the same time his sister did. "Look what we are getting to do today."

Lord Rollin's stony expression melted at once, and he smiled warmly at his children.

"Good day, children," he said, surveying the flowers that Henry showed him. "What is all this?"

Elizabeth gently pushed her brother out of the way to show their father her flowers.

"We are flower picking," she said. "Will you come join us? Please?"

Sophia recalled the afternoon of storytelling, and how Lord Rollins had rejected his children's pleas to stay a little longer. She bit her cheek, certain that he would be forced to similarly disappoint them yet again.

"I would be honoured to join you in your flower picking," he said, stroking the heads of both his children.

Sophia smiled, surprised. It seemed as though the viscount was taking more and more pleasure from spending time with his children in the recent weeks. And she could not have been more overjoyed. And yet, there was still a selfish part of her that was thrilled that she would get to spend time with him, as well. She tried not to let it show as she met her employer's gaze.

"Very well, then," she said. "Shall we move on to a different part of the garden?"

The children nodded, each of them taking one of their father's hands in their free ones.

"Yes, let us find Father's favourite flower," Elizabeth said.

Henry nodded.

"Yes," he said. "Father, what is your favourite flower?"

At this, the viscount paused. He thought it over for a long moment. Then, his eyes met Sophia's once more, and he gave her a slow smile that sent shivers down her spine.

"Red roses," he said. "Those are the most meaningful of all."

The connection between the pair returned, stealing Sophia's breath. And he nearly stole her heart's ability to beat when he fell into step beside her. She smiled up at him as the children skipped ahead, plucking clusters of honeysuckles and baby's breath to blend in with their bouquets. Sophia tried to focus on them and their surroundings, should she find something interesting to teach them or should they have any questions. But she found that the viscount kept gaining her attention. Especially when their hands brushed together as they walked along behind the children.

Her entire body jolted with awareness at the contact, and she looked up at him, fully expecting to see that it had been an accident and that he was coolly preparing a polite apology. But he was looking directly at her with his ever intensifying stare, and he gave her the smallest smirk that made her heart skip like mad. Then, he lifted his other hand and pointed at something to their right, just ahead of them.

It took Sophia a moment to collect herself and follow his finger. But by the time she had spotted a strange flower, the viscount had leaned in close to her, causing her cheeks to flood with heat and color and her heart to set off at a racehorse's pace.

"Do you see that flower?" he asked, his voice low and soft, the intimacy of which making Sophia's knees weak. "That is a rare orchid, available only in certain parts of the world. That was once my favourite flower." He paused, smiling. "But now, as you heard, it has changed to red roses, for passion and love."

Sophia felt that she might swoon as she looked at her employer's enchanting gaze. If there was more to the world than the two of them in that moment, she was unaware of it. What if there was a place in the world where they could love one another openly and without shame or fear? Was that truly such an impossible feat? Was there not some way they could have such a life?

A squeal pierced the air and broke the moment between them. They looked up to see Elizabeth pointing to a brilliant blue butterfly that flew past her head.

"Look," she said, jumping up and down. "That is the most beautiful shade of blue that I believe I have ever seen."

Sophia nodded.

"It is truly magnificent," she said. She looked at Lord Rollins, hoping to see a similar reaction from him. However, his face had changed, and he was looking up toward the manor. He quickly stepped away from her and directed his eyes to the ground.

"Excuse me," he said with no more than a polite nod. He dashed off away from them, disappearing before Sophia could understand what was happening.

"What happened?" Elizabeth asked, hurt shining in her eyes. "Did I upset Papa?"

Sophia shook her head though, in truth, she did not know what had happened.

"No, sweetheart," she said, offering a reassuring smile. "I think your father saw something that needed tending."

The girl nodded, but she looked as certain as Sophia felt. But before any of them could become any more upset or concerned with the matter, Sophia clapped her hands together and smiled.

"Let us finish gathering our bouquets, so that we can hurry and put them in vases for your new schoolroom," she said.

The children agreed, but with noticeably less enthusiasm than before. Still, Sophia kept her chipper expression, leading them toward the exit to the gardens. Only then did she glance up as Lord Rollins had, still pondering his sudden departure after such an intimate moment. She froze, feeling the color drain from her face. There in a second story window stood the dowager viscountess. And she was glowering at Sophia with hatred in her eyes. Sophia shuddered, fighting to keep the horror off her face as she led the children to the manor. Why was the lady of the house looking at her that way?

***

A governess's duties usually ended before the evening meal of every day. However, since the children had begun building such a strong bond with Sophia, she had taken to tucking in the children each night once Rebecca had them ready for bed. As she did so that night, her every thought was like an anchor, weighing down her mind and making it impossible to wrestle just one of them. She was tired, and yet she was sure she would be unable to sleep. Still, the comfort of her bed called to her, and she was ready to try to relax her body, if not her mind.

"Miss Hartley," a sharp voice hissed as she reached the landing that would take her to her chambers.

Sophia jumped, whirling around to find the dowager viscountess mere inches from her face. She stumbled backward, catching herself just before she fell onto her backside in front of the older woman.

"Yes, Lady Rollins?" she asked. She did not know what she had done to offend the woman. But she hoped to make it right quickly. As cold as Lord Rollins had initially been, his mother was far worse. It rattled Sophia terribly to be in her presence.

"I must remind you that you are nothing more than the governess here," she said. Her gaze was as pointed as her tone and the way she surveyed Sophia felt like Lady Rollins was observing a floor stain that desperately needed removing."

Sophia swallowed. What was prompting such malice?

"Yes, of course," she said. "I presume nothing else, I assure you."

The dowager snorted.

"Indeed," she said dryly. "I have seen the way you look at Julian. And any ideas you may have of having a life with him are purely and ridiculously fantasy."

Sophia shuddered. She cursed herself for having allowed her feelings for Lord Rollins show so freely on her face. She also chastised herself for putting herself in a position to run into him as often as she had been, and for encouraging him to spend more time with the children and her. Henry and Elizabeth required his attention. She, however, had no business hoping for it. And now, the dowager was reminding her of that fact.

"I would never think of hoping for a future with Lord Rollins," she said.

The dowager held up her hand, letting an icy silence linger

between the women. Then, she leaned in, much like the viscount had earlier that day, dropping her voice to a near inaudible level.

"Tread carefully, governess," she said, the letters trailing off into a long hiss. "You will find yourself dismissed from your position if I even think you are still entertaining such notions."

With that, the dowager turned, walking away from her with her head high. Sophia waited until she was out of sight, dashing to her chambers and locking the door. She collapsed onto her bed, her heart racing. She did not know what the dowager had seen or thought that she had. All that mattered was the last things she said. Her mother and Lucy depended too much on the income from her governess position for her to do anything to jeopardize it. She might have feelings for Lord Rollins. But even in the unlikely event that he shared those feelings, she would have to avoid him. Nothing was worth her risking her family's well-being. Not even the possibility of true love.

Chapter Twenty-two

Julian stands, smiling politely at all the picnic guests who are playing the various games that his mother arranged for them. Beside him is Lady Irene, chattering away about the lovely weather and the latest dresses in fashion within the ton. Julian is silent and brooding until his mother approaches.

"Irene, darling, your mother is looking for you," the dowager says.

Lady Irene looks perturbed, having just located Julian again after his return to the picnic, but she politely smiles at Augusta and Julian and curtseys, taking her leave. The dowager turns to Julian, giving him a pointed look.

"Irene's parents have noticed how you seem to be keeping her at a distance," she says. "And they witnessed you sneaking back to the picnic after vanishing for heaven knows how long. I do hope you have considered what I have said to you about your duties to our family and your station. Everyone is watching for you to make a good, suitable match. It is no secret that you have children who need you to have a good wife. You must never forget the importance of making a strong marriage match."

Julian nodded, bowing to his mother and concealing his anger with a passable smile.

"Of course, Mother," he said. "I will not forget."

And as he sat in his study, thinking about the picnic nearly a fortnight prior, he could not forget. But nor could he forget about the one woman who had managed to capture his attention and his interest.

Miss Hartley had been notably harder to encounter in the days since the picnic, and Julian and been concernedly disheartened. He had even stolen away to the gardens and the library on two separate days, hoping to catch the children and her, or even her on her own. But there had been no such luck. He had considered going to her chambers under the guise of calling a meeting to discuss the children's progress. But household employees loved nothing more than gossip, and he knew such a course of action would be noticed and spread.

Besides, he scolded himself, you know perfectly well that entertaining any unprofessional thoughts about serve no purpose. There is no sense in fooling yourself or leaving room for impropriety or scandal.

He did know those things. He could think of little else, especially since when he allowed his thoughts to wander freely, they always circled back to her and the lightning connection he felt with her when he looked in her eyes. He could not prevent the feelings that stirred within him. But nor could he allow them to surface to any part of the front of his mind. The difference in their stations would always prevent them from being anything more than they were. Even a friendship would be impossible for the two of them. And Julian had the impression that the feelings between them were far more than friends.

Julian stared up at the portrait of his wife, his heart heavy. It would not matter if it were Lady Irene, Miss Hartley or the second most beautiful woman in the ton. Nothing would alleviate the guilt he felt at even considering another woman in the place of his dear Eliza. He had sworn to love her until death parted them. And while it already had, his heart still clung to her and her memory as if his own life depended on it. Which was precisely how he felt it should remain.

A knock sounded at the door, pulling an irritated Julian from his thoughts. He looked up, preparing to bark an order for the intruder to leave him be and not disturb him again. But the door was open, which he had not noticed before. And stepping across the threshold was the only person, apart from Miss Hartley, that he truly wished to see.

"Good day, Julian," George said, carrying a thick stack of papers in his arms as he approached the desk. "I do hope you do not mind the last-minute intrusion. I have some documents that you and I should review."

Julian rose, motioning for his brother to sit. He fetched the whiskey, pouring each of them a glass as George rummaged through the papers and separating them into smaller packets.

"Your presence is never an intrusion, Brother," he said as he handed George one of the glasses. "What is that that you have there?"

George's eyes lit up with eager resolve as he grinned.

"I have news for you about our newest potential business ventures," he said.

Julian thought it over for a second while he sipped his drink. He had been so lost in thought that he feared that he had missed something with his brother. But he recalled how they had been talking about investing in some new local business, halving the cost of buying more land to rent and dabbling in scientific business pursuits. Then, he also smiled.

"Ah, yes," he said, gesturing to the multiple smaller stacks of papers. "Are we preparing to get our final affairs in order, as well?"

George gave Julian a mockery of a disgusted eye roll. Then, he handed Julian one of the document packets, looking like an excited puppy as Julian skimmed its contents.

"These are all the people with whom I have spoken about some of our ideas," he said. "There is also an itemised list of expenses we would incur to make each venture plausible from our end. And there is also a draft of the paper we will take to Father's attorney once we decide if we are going to move on one of these opportunities."

Julian flipped through the pages of one stack, picking up another and finding it held similar documents as the first.

"Very good, Brother," he said, smiling at George. "When can we begin?"

George's eyes sparkled and his grin widened.

"That is what I hoped you would say," he said.

Julian skimmed his way through the rest of the smaller packets that George had brought with him, making mental notes of the names on the lists that he had heard his father mention. He knew they worked with most of the late viscount's old partners. But he also knew there were some men with whom their father had wanted to work but had not gotten the chance when he was alive.

"You are far more organised than I, Brother," he said, almost envious.

George puffed out his chest, taking another sip of his drink.

"Which is why I never let you handle the important work," he said, unable to choke back his laughter.

Julian raised his eyebrows and nursed his own drink.

"Shall we get down to business, before feelings get too bruised?" he asked.

George blinked, his brow flinching to almost a furrow as he studied Julian. But then, he nodded, his smile returning.

"Certainly," he said. "You see there, on the page you are holding, I have also listed some prospects according not only to their reputations, but also to their approximate financial returns on their investments and ventures. I have also taken the liberty of listing the annual profits of each industry of interest to us on the last page of that packet."

Julian nodded, looking over the paper again. And yet, he was no longer reading the words written or listening to his brother. Instead, he was back in the gardens, telling his story to his children and the beautiful Miss Hartley, his mind sailing as far away from troubles as the prince sailed to catch up to the giants that had stolen the princess. He enjoyed discussing business with his brother, as there was never a dull moment, and together, they were always prosperous. But even such pleasant orders of business were invaded with thoughts of Miss Hartley of late. And he was certain that would only become truer as time passed.

"Julian?" George asked.

Julian shook his head, smiling at his brother when he realized that his face had drooped once more.

"I am listening," he said, leaning forward at something to which George was pointing.

His younger brother puckered his lips at Julian, giving his head a shake.

"Then you would know that I was not even holding this a moment ago," he said. "I picked it up to test your focus. And you failed horrifically. What is it that has you so preoccupied?"

Julian grimaced. He recalled the first conversation he and George had had about Miss Hartley. And he realized that he had done nothing but run from the possibility of ever having anything special with her because of the pressure his mother and Lord and Lady Locshire were putting on him to match with Lady Irene. He still had no intention of matching with her. But their insistence constantly reminded him that he was expected to marry a noblewoman. Not a governess.

But Julian was not ready to revisit that discussion right then. Not even with his understanding, comforting younger brother. He simply offered a big, reassuring smile and shook his head.

"I am fine, Brother," he said. "I have just been occupied with estate matters lately. It is nothing that will not pass."

George looked as unconvinced as Julian sounded unconvincing. The brothers stared at one another for a moment. Then, George nodded slowly. The disbelief was clear on his face, but it was equally apparent that he did not wish to press Julian.

"Very well," he said. "We shall discuss this another time. For now, we can proceed with these plans."

Julian nodded, feeling relieved despite knowing that George meant what he said about talking more about Julian's strange behavior lately. In truth, he would be glad to talk more. Just not right that moment.

"Excellent," Julian said, giving George another smile.

George grunted but said nothing further about Julian.

"As I was saying, I made a separate packet containing our current trade agreements," he said. "I thought that we could use these to shape any new ones that come along as we mark these prospects and potential partners off our list."

Julian nodded. With great effort, he put himself wholeheartedly back into the conversation.

"That is a wonderful idea, George," he said. "We should start planning meetings as soon as possible."

George smiled, the earlier doubt disappearing.

"Interesting that you should mention that," he said. "It so happens that we have a crucial meeting scheduled with someone who was very influential to Father's success in London in a few days. His support could very well ensure us a very profitable deal in the tea industry."

Julian's eyes lit up. He was not one for the boring monotony of business meetings. But when he and George attended them together, not only were they painless, but they also tended to gain important footholds in whichever industries and partnerships they sought. Besides, going into London would give him the chance to get away from their mother and, more importantly, Lady Irene. And, just maybe, he could garner some clarity on his feelings for the lovely, amazing governess.

"That is wonderful, Brother," he said. "When do we leave?"

George showed him another page, although he seemed now to be doing it solely out of habit.

"Tomorrow morning," he said. "I would like for us to be there early, so that we have plenty of time to prepare before the meeting."

Julian nodded eagerly, pouring each of them another drink.

"Splendid," he said. "Let us not waste any time making the preparations then, Brother."

Chapter Twenty-three

Sophia had made it a point to try to avoid Lord Rollins after the day of his picnic. She even went as far as to only take the children outside for short periods of time, only with Rebecca in their midst and when she was sure that Lord Rollins was either in a business meeting in his study or gone into town.

She enjoyed each moment he spent with her and the children, and she found herself wishing for more of them with each passing day. That was how she knew that avoiding him was what she had to do. But the less she saw of the viscount, the more she longed to see him. As her concerns about her family and the continued silence from her mother and sister grew, her thoughts became more troubled.

Then one morning, about two weeks after encountering her employer in the gardens during the dowager's and his picnic, Sophia was awakened by a knock at the door. She opened it to reveal a solemn-faced Wyatt.

"Forgive my unorthodox intrusion, Miss Hartley," he said, holding out a letter. "I felt this was urgent enough that it could not wait. This came for you just now, and the man who delivered it passed along the message that it is of the gravest importance."

Sophia's heart fell even before she glanced down at the envelope. It was from Lucy, she knew immediately from the script, although the letters were shaky, and the ink appeared to be smeared in places. A lump formed in her throat, but she gave the butler her best kind smile.

"Thank you kindly, Wyatt," she said.

The butler bowed, vanishing down the hallway. Sophia closed the door, ripping open the letter before she even sat down at her desk.

Sophia,

I have terrible news. Mother had fallen deathly ill. She had taken to shutting herself in her room, and three nights ago I went inside to take her breakfast. She was pale and weak and not responding to any efforts to rouse her. I ran outside and shouted for help, and Mrs. Smith from down the street came to our aid. She tended Mother for one night, finally bringing her to consciousness. But she could not stay as she has children to feed, leaving me to tend Mother as best I can. However, Mother grows weaker and less talkative with each passing day, and my resources for caring for her are already dangerously thin.

Please, come home. I am frightened, and we cannot yet afford for me to send for a physician. I am doing everything I can for Mother, but I fear it will not be enough. I need your help, Sister. I apologise for making such a request, and I assure you that I would not do so if I did not truly believe that things were so dire. But I need you, Sophie. Please, come as quickly as you can. I believe that Mother will not survive.

Lucy

The lack of loving signature and the fact that Lucy had called her Sophie, which she had not done since she was four, frightened Sophia to her core. Tears were streaming down her cheeks and falling down on top of the splatters that she was now sure were Lucy's own teardrops covering the page. Sophia's heart was destroyed. How could she ever choose between the sweet, reliant children who had come to trust her role and her presence in their lives and her own mother and sister? She had responsibilities to both, and she could never force herself to place one above the other in her heart.

I cannot possibly neglect the children now, she thought, wiping tears from her face even as she shook more of them free from her eyes with her sobs. I made them a promise that I would always be here for them, and they need that to be true. But nor can I leave mother to agonize in her ailment and Lucy to fret and lament in the situation all alone without me being there to help them. Heavens, what shall I do?

She thought back to what Rebecca had said. Her brother and father had been incapacitated, nearly simultaneously, and yet they had both recovered and gone on to live normally once again. But from the sound of the letter, it did not seem that Caroline Hartley would have the time to wait and see if her condition improved in such a fashion.

Once again, Sophia thought about how Rebecca had managed to return home to help her family and still retain her job, and how Sophia herself did not have such an option. She also thought about how she would be hurting and disappointing someone, no matter which choice she made. Sophia could never forgive herself for abandoning any of the people she loved. But how was she supposed to make the right decision?

As Sophia stared at the letter, which was slowly becoming more crumpled in her hands, she realized there was no choice. There was only one correct answer to her dilemma. No matter how much it hurt her to make such a decision.

"I must go to Mother and Lucy," she said softly to herself, sobbing aloud as she spoke to the empty room. "My life here has been beautiful. But it would be nothing without Mother, and Lucy is too young to watch her die alone."

At the notion of Caroline dying, Sophia choked on a horrible round of sobs. She fought to catch her breath, unsuccessful on her first few attempts. But as soon as she could draw air into her lungs, she forced herself to breathe. She was about to do the hardest thing she had ever done. And she had to try to be calm, even as her heart broke into delicate, flaking pieces.

She pulled paper from the desk, smoothing it with trembling hands across the surface. She dipped the feather quill into the ink well, glaring at her unsteady fingers as if she could force them to stop their trembling. Then, she began to write.

Dearest Lucy,

Do not fret. I will pack up my things and leave for home first thing. I know things must seem dire now, and I cannot imagine how frightened and worried you are. But you are strong, and I know that you will be all right—

Realizing what she was doing, she wadded up the letter and tossed it into the bin. She would arrive at their apartment long before the letter ever did. It would be foolish to waste time writing to her sister, when she should be packing up her things. However, she did take a fresh sheet of stationery out of the desk. There was one letter she had to write. Only it was not to her mother or sister.

Dear Lord Rollins,

It is with the heaviest of hearts that I write you this letter. I must end my tenure here at Rollins Manor effective immediately, as my mother has fallen deathly ill. My sister has been caring for her during my employment here. However, at merely twelve years old, she is not yet ready to handle the events which she detailed to me in her latest letter.

I assure you that this decision was not made lightly. My heart breaks at having to leave your employ, as your family has become very special to me, as has my position as governess. However, I must leave to take care of my own family, as I am the only one whom they have left.

I am closing this letter to say goodbye to both Henry and Elizabeth. I shall not leave them believing that they did anything wrong to make me leave.

I will miss you all dearly. I hope this does not put your family in a bind, needing a replacement for me on such short notice.

Please, forgive me, Lord Rollins.

Sincerely,

Sophia Hartley

She shook the letter to try to dry the tear-stains that dotted the page. Then, she hastily folded it, tucking it into the pocket of her uniform. She hurried out of her chambers, rushing downstairs in the hopes of running into Mrs. Barnes. She did, just as she was headed to the kitchens to see if the cook had seen her. The housekeeper started to greet her with a smile. But when she saw Sophia's wet cheeks, her brow wrinkled with concern.

"What is wrong, darling?" she asked.

Sophia shook her head, thrusting the letter into the housekeeper's hands.

"I am afraid that I must go," she said. "Please, see to it that Lord Rollins gets this letter. And no one else. You may read it if you wish. But I need to know that he will get it."

Mrs. Barnes' eyes were wide with alarm. But she merely nodded, putting her note in her apron and embracing Sophia firmly.

"I will miss you, dear," she whispered.

Sophia pulled away and nodded.

"I will miss you all," she said, choking on more sobs.

Next, she returned to her chambers, gathering her meager possessions as quickly as she could. As she closed her trunk, the necklace with the portrait of her father slipped from the neckline of her dress. She reached for it, tracing it with her fingertips.

Father, I would give anything for your comfort and reassurance now, she thought as more emotions rolled in, threatening to drown her. *I do not know if I can do this for all three of us on my own.*

She had not expected her father to answer her silent plea. However, when no answer came to her, it still elicited more sobs from her aching chest. Still, she collected herself once more, leaving her chambers for two more important errands.

First, she scoured the halls until she found Lady Rollins, who was taking tea in her parlor. She shuddered as she recalled the hateful message the dowager had whispered to her, threatening her position if she did not leave Lord Rollins alone. Perhaps, Lady Rollins would not be so harsh, seeing as she was getting her way with Sophia's departure, without having to explain why she had terminated her position.

"Lady Rollins?" Sophia asked, her voice cracking.

The dowager looked up, her green eyes colder than Sophia had ever seen Julian's.

"May I help you?" she asked, her voice clipped and sharper than a barber's blade.

Sophia swallowed, briefly explaining the need to depart and the reasons why.

The dowager waved at her dismissively before she finished speaking, and Sophia was strangely relieved.

"Fine," Lady Rollins said without a shred of compassion or remorse. "You are easy enough to replace."

Sophia turned and fled, not waiting to see if the dowager would speak again. It took her several moments to put herself back together yet again. Then, she headed for the nursery.

Like Mrs. Barnes, Rebecca first smiled upon noticing Sophia enter. But also like the housekeeper, her face became filled with worry when she noticed the tears. Sophia held up her hand, motioning for the children, who were playing with Henry's toy soldiers, to join her and the nursemaid near the door.

"My darlings," she said, embracing them both so tightly that she could have taken their breath. "I am afraid that I must leave you."

The other three people in the room gasped in unison, donning matching expressions of horror.

"Why?" Rebecca breathed, putting her hand to her chest.

Elizabeth shook her head, tears already forming in her green eyes.

"No, please," she said, her words giving way to a wail. "You cannot leave us."

Henry sniffled and hiccuped, evidently trying to hold back his own sobs.

"You cannot leave," he echoed. "You promised."

A loud sob escaped Sophia's own throat, causing the children to cry harder. She held them tightly to her, rubbing their backs, trying vainly to comfort them.

"I do not want to leave," she said. "But I must."

Rebecca put a hand on Sophia's shoulder, shaking her head.

"But why, darling?" she asked.

Sophia took a futile breath, explaining as she had to Mrs. Barnes the reasons why she was leaving. By the end of her explanation, the children were both hysterical, clinging to her arms and skirts and refusing to let her go.

"Please," Elizabeth said again. "We love you. You can go and see your mother and then come back to us."

Sophia looked into the children's innocent, red eyes and her heart shattered. They had grown to love her just as she had grown to love them. And now, she was taking away the one bond that had given them the confidence and inspiration to grow and flourish. She did not know if she could ever forgive herself.

"I am so sorry, sweet darlings," she said, burying her face in their hair. "Please, forgive me."

She held the children and allowed them to cry a moment longer. Then, Rebecca, the kind soul that she was, gently put her hands on each of their shoulders. She gave Sophia a kind, warm smile and a nod, gesturing to the door behind Sophia with her eyes.

"Come, sweet ones," she said in the kindest voice. "Let us clean up your toys and get ready for bed a little early. I shall read you a while longer tonight, if you like."

The despondent children said nothing as they eventually allowed the nursemaid to pull their small hands from Sophia's dress. Rebecca turned to lead them back to where they had been playing, but Elizabeth looked back over her shoulder.

"I love you, Miss Hartley," she said, whimpering as she spoke.

Sophia covered her mouth to keep her own hysteria at bay.

"And I love you, precious children," she said, nearly choking on the lump in her throat.

After another long, agonizing moment, Sophia turned and left the room. She could hear the wailing begin again, and she, too, started to cry once more. She hurried to the nearest maid, requesting a hackney to be hired to take her to London immediately. Then, she fetched her own trunks, toting them down the stairs, where Wyatt helped her take them outside.

"Mrs. Barnes told me," was all the butler said to her.

Sophia nodded, giving him a weak smile.

"Goodbye, Wyatt," she whispered.

A short time later, the hackney arrived, pulling her away from the place she had known as home for the past few weeks. She did not dare look out the window until Rollins Manor was long out of sight. As she watched the scenery slowly turn from wildflowers and fields to buildings and other coaches, her heart grew heavier and heavier. She already regretted leaving her new, albeit dearly, beloved ones. The sadness was almost too great for her to bear, and it was all she could do to control another bout of sobbing. She was not remorseful for doing what her mother and sister needed her to do. She only wished that she had not had to sacrifice love to do it.

Love, she thought with a bittersweet smile as she thought about Lord Rollins. A love that shall never be allowed to blossom, forever to remain nothing more than a memory.

She sighed. It was true that she would never get to be with the viscount in the way she had foolishly allowed herself to dream. However, there would be time enough to lament the loss later. Right then, the only thing that mattered, the only thing that could matter, was her family. She had to reach them in time to help her mother. And she needed to be strong, no matter what was to come. Lucy would depend on her strength, just as she had relied on their father's. And she could not let anything distract her from that purpose.

Chapter Twenty-four

After three days of meetings, discussions and document drafting, Julian returned home at last. It had been a grueling endeavor, exhausting Julian through and through. However, he and George had managed to successfully get through the negotiations for which they set off for London. His head ached and his body cried for proper rest, but Julian felt satisfied at the end of the business dealings.

He and George had spoken with some old partners of their father's and secured a deal in the technology industry that would bring prosperity to their family for many years to come. Specifically, scientific and medical technology. It was something in which their father had expressed an interest, and something which the brothers had been researching. Despite the tension between his mother and him recently, Julian was eager to speak with his mother and give her the wonderful news.

However, he was met with a stony silence as he entered the front door of Rollins Manor. He shivered, despite the warmth of the day, feeling as though an invisible but dark cloud had settled over him. Wondering at the feeling of seemingly unfounded dread, he bid Wyatt a good day and headed down the grand foyer. As he reached the end of it, he found himself face to face with Mrs. Barnes. Her lips were pressed tightly together, and her expression was solemn and serious.

"Lord Rollins," she said, sadness and concern evident in her words as she handed him a letter she held tightly in her hand. "You must read this at once. Things seem to be quite dire, I am afraid."

Julian raised an eyebrow as he took the letter.

"What has happened?" he asked, carefully unfolding the wrinkled letter.

Mrs. Barnes sighed, shaking her head.

"It's Miss Hartley," she said.

Julian's heart dropped. Had something terrible happened to Miss Hartley? Was she ill, or had she suffered some horrible accident? His mind raced, even as he held the answers in his hands. He did not bother to hide his worry as he turned his eyes to the page. He quickly scanned the note, which was written in beautiful but shaky script, squinting to read the letters that were smudged, seemingly by moisture. And as he deciphered the hastily scribbled letter, his heart made its way from his stomach to his throat.

"No," he whispered, rereading the letter. "No."

Miss Hartley had detailed the sorrowful tale of her gravely ill mother and frightened, twelve-year-old sister who was being forced to care for the ailing woman on her own with limited resources. The governess was incredibly apologetic, informing him also that she had bade the children farewell, so that they did not think that her leaving was in any way their fault.

As tears threatened to fill Julian's eyes, he understood what the moisture spots on the page were. They were tears. Miss Hartley had been crying as she wrote the words, and apparently quite hard, indicating the immense distress she had been experiencing as she tried to write. Yet even with her evident trauma, she had still cared enough about his children to speak to them and not leave them with unfounded sorrow and unanswered questions.

I love her, he thought, not attempting to cease the thought as it crossed his mind. He was too shocked and frightened to try to filter his thoughts through the filters of societal expectations. I love her, and she desperately needs help.

With his head down, still staring at the letter, which he was no longer reading, Julian turned around abruptly, bumping right into his mother. He did not spare her a glance, moving to step around her. Whatever she wanted, it would have to wait until he was ready. But she did not allow him to sidestep her. Instead, she blocked his path until, annoyed and distressed, he glowered at her and sighed.

"What is it, Mother?" he asked.

For a moment, she looked bewildered, as though she had no idea what was happening. Julian wondered if Miss Hartley had explained herself to Augusta before leaving. If she had not, would he end up with his mother hating her far more than she already did?

The dowager looked down at the letter clasped tightly in his fist. A cold sort of understanding crossed her face, and she gave Julian an impatient sneer.

"I suppose that is from the most recent former governess," she said, not bothering to take a proper look and confirm for herself. "That is what I came to tell you. She quit."

Julian stared at her in disbelief. In that instant, he saw every situation in which he had been cold and callused, uncaring and aloof. He was flooded with guilt, but he dammed it up quickly with the more important matter at hand.

"Do you even understand why?" he asked.

Augusta shrugged, looking as disinterested as Julian worked to make himself look and act. Even around his own children until recently. Until Sophia Hartley, he thought, all the pieces falling into place.

"Something about a family illness," she said. "Honestly, I do wonder what it is about the families of governesses that renders so many of them unable to complete their full tenure with an employer."

Julian shook his head.

"How can you be so cruel?" he asked.

His mother looked at him, raising her eyebrow and narrowing her eyes.

"You always did look at that girl in a most unhealthy way," she said. "And do not think I did not notice how you kept managing to encounter her around the property. You clearly believed that you felt something for her. But she was merely a young lady from a very poor family who saw her chance to take everything she could get from a very wealthy, reputable gentleman. And there is no telling what else she might have done if she had stayed here in our employ."

Julian stared dumbly at his mother. His anger with her was genuine, and it might have been impossible to not speak with such a scalding emotion, were it not for the fact that a realization crashed the high tide shores of his mind.

"No, Mother," he said, holding up his hand and setting his

jaw firmly. "That is what Lady Irene was. Sophia is warm and caring, she dotes on the children as though they were her very own and she had never done anything except for every single thing she was expected to do. She even went above and beyond when it was in the best interest of Henry and Elizabeth. I daresay she loved them every bit as much as Eliza did."

Augusta Rollins looked as though Julian had struck her. She stared at him, horrified, her lips moving silently for a moment.

"You cannot believe that woman had any genuine interest in caring for Henry and Elizabeth," she said. "She came her with no experience, reeking of desperation and with nefarious intentions in her eyes."

Julian moved a step closer to his mother, narrowing his eyes.

"You will never speak of her that way again, Mother," he said. "In fact, you will never speak of her at all if you are willing to be so nasty now. You failed to see the horrid woman that Lady Irene is. Just as you fail to see how pure and sincere Miss Hartley is. I have said all that I have to say on this matter. I love Miss Hartley, and I am going to her. And not you nor anyone else in the whole world will stop me. Is that clear?"

The dowager was once more speechless. Only this time, Julian did not give her the chance to regain her words. He stormed past her, summoning Wyatt and standing rigidly until the butler appeared.

"Ready a carriage to London at once," he said.

Wyatt did not ask any questions. He vanished, leaving Julian to wait blissfully alone while the preparations were made. Less than half an hour later, his carriage was ready, and he ran out the front door. His mother tried calling after him about how he was making a mistake. But he did not break stride or so much as look toward the manor until the carriage reached the end of the carriage-way. You wanted the children to have a mother, Mother, he thought. Now, it is I who knows just who that mother should be.

During the whole trip to Miss Hartley's home, Julian's heart pounded in his chest. He did not know if she would be glad to see him, but he hoped he could give her reason to be. He understood that she might not be willing to accept charity. However, help with her mother was not all that he intended to offer her. He had spoken the truth to his mother. And he planned to tell that to the woman who needed to hear it the most.

After what seemed to him like days, he was tumbling out of the carriage before it came to a stop in front of the building which housed Miss Hartley's family's apartment. He raced directly to her door, knocking frantically and hoping she would see him. To his relief, she opened the door, her eyes growing wide with surprise, rather than horror.

"Lord Rollins," she breathed. Her face was alarmingly pale, and her eyes were red with dark circles beneath them. It was clear that she had not been sleeping, and his heart broke. "Please, do come in."

Julian smiled, relieved.

"Thank you," he said. "I received your note. Tell me, how is your mother doing?"

Her lip trembled, and it took her a moment to compose herself. Julian wanted desperately to take her in his arms and hold her. However, he simply put his hand on hers and waited in patient silence for her to answer.

"It is even worse than I feared," she said, her words shaking as her mouth did. "Her mind is very foggy, and she had an alarmingly high fever. I have tried everything I know to bring it down. But it only went down once, my first few hours back home. Since then, it only seems to gradually increase."

Miss Hartley was breathing heavily, near hysterics, by the time she finished explaining the situation to Julian. He could not bear to see her in such a state of distress, so he quickly found a solution.

"I shall send my physician to her," he said gently. "I will spare no expense and I will pay for any and all treatment. She will get everything she needs to get well again. And I shall see to it that you and your family receive any supplies and food you need during this time of crisis. You, your mother and sister shall want or need for nothing while your mother recovers. And I will not hear a word of protest."

Miss Hartley stared at him for several moments, clearly

trying to understand what he had said to her. Then, she sobbed, but her trembling lips were replaced by a wide smile as she put her hands to her cheeks.

"Truly?" she asked. "You would do this for my family and me?" She paused, shaking her head in disbelief. "But why?"

Julian took her hands in his, giving her a timid smile as he softly wiped away the tears streaming down her cheeks.

"Because I love you," he said, his smile widening as the walls that had separated them since he first met her came tumbling down. "I have loved you since I first met you, and now, I cannot go one more day trying to pretend that I do not." He tried to clear the raw emotion from his voice, but he failed. So, he simply settled for swallowing a lump in his throat and waiting nervously for her response.

She looked at him, giving him the chance to witness her eyes filling with wonder and delight. He knew what she would say before she spoke, and yet the words still set his heart into super flight.

"And I have loved you, as well," she said. "I never dreamed that you felt the same. But now that I know that you do, I hardly have words for how much joy I feel."

Julian cupped her face tenderly in his hands. He leaned in, giving the woman he loved, who he now knew loved him, a sweet, loving kiss.

"Now, let us get your mother the help she needs," he said.

Sophia beamed at him, all the worry that had lined her beautiful face vanishing in seconds.

"Thank you, my love," she said.

Chapter Twenty-five

"Darling, would you mind reading a little more?" Caroline Hartley said, smiling hopefully at her eldest daughter.

Sophia giggled, nodding happily.

"I would be delighted, Mother," she said.

She turned the page to Pride and Prejudice, the book she had been reading to Henry and Elizabeth before she had had to leave to return home, beginning the next chapter. Her voice was warm and comforting, but inside she was filled with a delight she had never hoped to feel again just days prior. Rather than fear and anxiety as she sat at her mother's bedside, the atmosphere was now filled with tranquility and reassurance.

Caroline, who had been so near death just a few days ago, now sat up in bed, smiling, an empty bowl which had held a hearty helping of veal stew on her bedside table and a jacket, which she had been working on mending before she fell ill, laying across her lap, abandoned as Sophia read gently to her. It was a more miraculous recovery than Sophia had dared to hope for, and it was all she could do to contain her thrilled relief.

Sophia knew that if it had not been for Julian and his kind generosity in sending the physician and providing ample money for food during those few days, she almost certainly would have lost her mother. But now, that trouble was behind her and she could hardly stop smiling. Even Lucy was every bit the youthful, exuberant girl that Sophia had remembered during her first days working at Rollins Manor, once it was evident that their mother would survive. She bounced around the house, humming loudly as she performed the chores and took her turns looking after Caroline.

As Sophia turned another page, her energetic little sister bound through the door, her cheeks pink, and her eyes wide with joy.

"Sophia," she said, dancing in the doorway. "We have guests."

Sophia's brow furrowed, but her sister's smile was infectious, and she returned it.

"Guests?" she asked. "Who?"

Lucy grinned impishly, motioning for Sophia to follow her.

"Come and see," she said.

Sophia laughed again, looking at their mother.

"Go on, sweetheart," she said, casting a knowing glance at her younger daughter. "You must never keep company waiting."

Sophia nodded, setting aside the book. Her heart skipped as a hopeful thought crossed her mind. Was it possible that Julian had come to call on them?

She followed her sister back to the living room of the small apartment, giggling once more at the prance in Lucy's walk. For the first time since their father died, their home did not feel burdened with grief and stress. And Sophia believed that she could not be happier.

When they turned toward the doorway that led into the living room, however, Sophia's heart leapt for joy. Her steps hastened when she heard very familiar, and most welcomed, voices. Those of Henry and Elizabeth. And as they entered the room, Sophia's eyes instantly met those of Julian, his intense, loving gaze rendering her as speechless as it did breathless.

"Miss Hartley," both children said in unison, the pure delight radiating from their voices. They rushed over to her, throwing their arms around her, much as they had when she had told them she must leave them to help her sick mother. This time, however, there were brilliant smiles on their faces, and there was joy in their eyes.

"Oh, darlings," Sophia said, stooping to embrace them both. "I have missed you dearly.

The children clung to her for a moment before pulling away.

"How is your mother?" Henry asked?

Sophia smiled warmly at him, touched by his concern and compassion.

"She is feeling much better," she said, looking up at Julian. "And all because of your father."

Julian approached then, giving Sophia a doting smile.

"It overjoys me to hear that your mother is doing well," he

said. "And how are you?"

Sophia blushed, smiling up at him before glancing at the children.

"I do not think I have ever felt better," she said, looking at him again.

Julian nodded as he brushed a strand of hair from her face.

"That is wonderful," he said. Then, he looked at Lucy, who was silently vibrating with excitement behind Sophia. "And this must be your sister, Miss Lucy Hartley."

Lucy grinned, rushing forward. Then, she remembered herself and curtseyed.

"It is a pleasure to meet you, Lord Rollins," she said.

Julian chuckled.

"There is no need for such formality, Miss Lucy," he said.

The children approached Lucy with wide, confident smiles. Sophia marveled again at how far they had come from the shy, reserved children she had first met. She stood back to witness them introduce themselves to Lucy.

"I am Henry Rollins," Henry said, bowing just like his father did.

Elizabeth curtseyed, giggling when Lucy did again, as well.

"And I am Elizabeth," she said.

Lucy smiled at the children, winking at Sophia.

"It is lovely to meet both of you, as well, Master Henry and Miss Elizabeth," she said.

The children giggled wildly at the formal manner of address.

"There is no need for such formality," Elizabeth said, echoing her father's words through her laughter.

Lucy nodded, giving the children a playfully serious look.

"Oh, well, then what shall I call you?" she asked.

Henry and Elizabeth began laughing again and Henry shook his head.

"Henry and Elizabeth, silly," he said. "And we shall call you Lucy."

Lucy gasped, pretending to be suddenly enlightened.

"Why, of course," she said. "That sounds perfect to me."

The children, still laughing reached out and hugged Lucy. She looked briefly surprised before returning their embrace. She shared a look with her older sister that told Sophia that she was touched. Sophia herself felt her heart grow warmer still at the sight.

Julian touched her shoulder, looking on as Henry and Elizabeth interacted with Lucy.

"I can see that you truly did do a wonderful job helping your sister," he said, looking down at her fondly. "Although truthfully, I knew it from the very first moment I saw you with the children."

Sophia blushed.

"Lucy is a wonderful young lady," she said modestly. "And Henry and Elizabeth are wonderful children. A governess is only as good as her charges, I believe."

Julian's smile widened and he shook his head.

"Such humility," he said softly. "Just one of so many reasons why I knew you were special."

Sophia's cheeks burned as Julian took her hands in his, much like the day when he had professed his love for her. The gesture was so gentle that it sent shivers down her spine. Suddenly, the intensity in his eyes burned hotter than it ever had before. His expression was kind and loving, but serious and, she thought, hopeful and apprehensive.

He cleared his throat, holding the silently intent gaze a moment longer. When he spoke again, he did so with more emotion than she had ever heard from anyone.

"Sophia, I told you that I loved you, and I have never been more sincere with words that I spoke," he said. "But there is one thing which I did not say, one thing which cannot wait a moment longer."

Sophia blinked, her head shaking gently in confusion.

"I do not understand," she said. "What is it?"

Julian looked down at their intertwined hands, taking a deep, shaky breath. He was nervous, to be sure. But why?

"I love you in a way I never believed I could love again," he said. "And the more time that passes without you by my side, the more my heart aches for you. The days without you have been among the darkest of my life. And I do not wish to spend another night in such black emptiness. I cannot imagine my life without you in it. Permanently."

Sophia's breath caught. Was he saying what she thought he was saying? Or was she getting too far ahead of herself.

"Julian, I feel the same about you," she said. "I never expected to find love and kinship when I began in your employ. But now, my life is all the richer for knowing you and the children, and I cannot picture any future where I do not know your love and companionship."

Julian smiled at her, squeezing her hands.

"You have brought more joy into our lives than I could have ever dared to hope was possible," he said. "Please, tell me that you will agree to be my wife."

The entire room fell silent, apart from Sophia's pounding heart. He was saying exactly what she had thought, what she had hoped. She was overwhelmed, and she struggled to find the words she desperately sought.

"Mother, come quickly," Lucy said, shouting as she raced down the hall.

Sophia laughed through joy filled tears, grateful for the intermission. She heard her sister yell something else as she banged open the door to Caroline's room once more, and although Sophia did not hear what it was, she was sure she could accurately guess. Sophia used the delay to collect herself. She had once believed that she, a lowly nobleman's employee, could never be good enough to marry him. Did she still believe that? Or did she truly believe that they could have the happy family she had seen in her dreams?

Slowly, Lucy guided their mother into the living room. Caroline Hartley's eyes were filled with tears as she took a seat in their rocking chair.

"Go on," Lucy prompted once their mother was settled. "Answer him, Sister."

Sophia giggled again, turning back to Julian. She had her word. And she could not wait to say it.

"Yes," she said, laughing as shock overtook Julian's face. "Yes, Julian, I will marry you."

The silence that had claimed the rest of the room ended with applause and shrieks of delight and joy. The children squealed, jumping up and down and embracing one another. Lucy giggled wildly, clapping her hands, and bouncing as excitedly as the children. Even Caroline rose to her feet, sobbing with joy as she embraced her daughter and future son-in-law.

"Oh, heavens," she said, her voice stronger than Sophia had heard it in days. "I could not be more thrilled this day."

The children interrupted the embrace with one of their own. They were still squealing, and Sophia had never been more enthralled with their voices.

"Does this mean that you will be our new mother?" Henry asked.

Sophia looked at Julian, who nodded.

"Yes," she said. "But I know that you loved your mother dearly, and that you always will. You need not call me Mother. You may simply call me Sophia."

The children looked quite pleased with her answer. They shared a look, then Elizabeth smiled sweetly up at her.

"Very well, Sophia," she said. "We cannot wait until you become our new mother."

Julian beamed at her with pride, stroking her cheek.

"And I cannot wait for you to become my wife," he said.

Sophia laughed giddily at those two words. Wife and mother were dreams she had given up months ago. Now, she would get to be both, and it was even better than she had imagined.

"And now, I get a brother," Lucy said, laughing as she leapt into her sister's arms. "And a wonderful niece and nephew, as well."

Sophia held her sister tightly, both their faces lit with happiness. The sisters had tears of equal joy running down their cheeks. And Sophia understood then that sometimes, the princess really did turn out to be a mere governess.

Epilogue

Lucy was a whirlwind in the weeks following Julian's proposal. She flitted about the dress shops of London with her older sister, critiquing each fabric and shade of white that was available to them. Julian had told Sophia to select whatever she wished for their wedding. He invested a hefty sum in the affair, granting Sophia the ability to plan the wedding she had dreamed of having since she was Lucy's age.

Caroline, who was still recovering from some lingering fatigue from her illness, spent much of her time at home, working on dresses for Lucy and herself for the wedding. Susan Rollins, Julian's sister-in-law, was a terrific godsend. She stepped into the role that the dowager viscountess would have taken, were she not so distant since Julian's declaration of love for his now former governess. Sophia had not seen nor heard from Lady Rollins since the day she departed to care for her mother. It was the one dark cloud over what was otherwise the happiest and most overwhelming time in her life.

One week before the wedding, Susan accompanied Lucy and Sophia to the seamstress for Sophia's final dress fitting. Lucy was, as ever, beside herself, darting around the shop and pointing out accessories and commenting on the seamstress's work and skill. As Sophia stood before the mirror, her breath caught in her chest. Having been the daughter of a wealthy merchant, she had often had nice dresses to wear. But for the first time in almost two years, she felt like a princess.

"Oh, Sophia, darling," Susan said, squeezing her hand gently, careful not to jar Sophia or bump into the seamstress, who was deftly putting pins around the hem of the dress. "I have never seen a more beautiful bride."

Lucy nodded her agreement with tears in her eyes.

"Sister, your dress could not be more perfect," she said.

Sophia nodded. It was still difficult for her to fathom that her life had changed so drastically in such a short time, and then changed again even more quickly. She had gone from a loving daughter to a grieving one, from a wealthy young lady to a poor one, and now, she was to be viscountess to her beloved and cherished viscount, Julian. She and her family would be cared for from then on, and they would never have to worry about money ever again.

"I believe that life could not be more perfect," she said, pushing aside the darkness that was the rift between herself and her future mother-in-law.

Then, on the night before the wedding, a miracle occurred. There was a knock on the door as Caroline put the final changes on the dresses. Sophia was finishing the pig roast she made for dinner, so Lucy raced to answer the unexpected visitor. When she raced in the kitchen with wide, bewildered eyes, Sophia's heart stopped.

"Come quickly," she said in a hushed voice. "It is Lady Rollins."

Sophia swallowed. Why had the dowager come to visit her at home? Had she come alone? Had Julian sent her, or was she there on her own accord? And why?

Sophia collected herself, gesturing for Lucy to take over looking after the roast. She went to the living room, where the dowager was waiting for her.

"Miss Hartley," she said, dipping her head. "I would like to speak with you. May I have a moment of your time?"

Sophia forced a smile and nodded.

"Of course," she said. "Please, come in."

The dowager nodded, following Sophia over to the small, worn sofa in the living room. Sophia expected her to make a sour face or refuse to sit down. Instead, however, she merely looked sad as she took the spot beside Sophia.

"I wanted to apologise," she said, not wasting a moment.

Sophia stared blankly at Lady Rollins. She was unsure what was happening, but she could not help feeling nervous, despite what the dowager had just said. She had not forgotten the conversation she had with Lady Rollins about Julian and how she needed to leave him be. Yet she would have never thought that the dowager might be remorseful for that. She had made it perfectly clear what she thought of Sophia. Why would that change now?

"For what, my lady?" she asked timidly.

The dowager sighed.

"I admit that I had certain prejudices about social status and stations," she said. "I treated you very poorly because of those prejudices, mistakenly thinking that things simply must be a certain way. I said horrible things to you, treating you like you were less than a person."

Sophia continued looking at Lady Rollins with wide eyes. She was uncertain what she should say, so she nodded, scrambling for words.

"I am aware of the expectations of our social classes," she said. "My father was a very wealthy merchant, and even amongst merchant families, there seemed to be an unspoken division between those like my father and those who made less in their industry."

It was Lady Rollins' turn to stare. She shook her head, her remorse becoming more evident on her face.

"Oh, dear," she said. "I had no idea you came from wealth."

Sophia gave her a small smile.

"It is all right," she said. "I only mentioned it to Julian once. After Father died, it hardly seemed as important to me as it perhaps once was."

The dowager nodded, biting her lip.

"I cannot say that would have changed my behaviour toward you when I first noticed my son's interest in you," she said. "However, what I came to tell you now is that status should not matter. You are poised, refined, courteous, kind, compassionate and delightful. You have made my son and grandchildren happier than I ever dared hope they could be again after Eliza died. Frankly, I misjudged and ridiculed you and for that, I am truly very sorry."

Sophia's heart leapt. She had hoped that the dowager might come to accept her marriage to Julian, if only for the sake of her relationship with her son. However, for Lady Rollins to work so intently to make amends with Sophia, she now hoped they could find happiness as a whole family.

"It is all right, Lady Rollins," she said again. "I assure you that all is forgiven."

The dowager reached out and took her hands as relief washed over her expression.

"Thank you, darling," she said. "But please, call me Augusta. I could not be more delighted to be considered at least a friend to you and, perhaps one day, family."

Overwhelmed with joy, Sophia embraced her future mother-in-law.

"As far as I am concerned, you are already family, Augusta," she said.

***

The following day, Caroline Hartley walked arm in arm with Sophia down the aisle of the chapel. Sophia felt more like royalty in her dress of ivory silk than she had on the day the seamstress had taken it in on her final fitting. Her mother was sobbing beside her, walking slowly but with strong, sure footsteps as the dearest loved ones of both Sophia and Julian smiled at her from the pews. Ahead of her, next to the vicar, stood Julian, in the most handsome midnight blue suit that Sophia had ever seen. His dark brown hair was perfectly combed and parted down the middle, the front pieces on either side of the part resting just above his green eyes, which were filled with love and tears.

As Sophia reached the man she was marrying, he took her arm, giving her mother a kiss on the cheek. Lucy rose from her seat to help Caroline to the spot beside her and Sophia and Julian turned to face the vicar. But in the instant before her gaze met the clergy's, Sophia saw Augusta. Her smile was warm and wider than she had ever witnessed, and there were tears in her eyes. Sophia winked at her, then readied herself for the ceremony to officially begin.

The exchange of vows was the most thrilling moment of Sophia's life. She understood that Julian had done it once before. But when she saw the utter devotion and sincerity with which he spoke them to her, she had no doubt that he was as in love with her as she was with him. She smiled at him, reciting the vows back to him with delighted anxiety when it was her turn. It was a beautiful ceremony. However, the best part was the last, and Sophia awaited it with joy.

As the vicar introduced them as the Viscount and the new Viscountess Rollins, her heart sang. She smiled through happy tears, her hand trembling with joy as she signed the registry alongside her new husband. She had told Julian that she never would have imagined that life as a governess could bring her so much joy, and she had been sincere. Now, the real bliss could begin in her new life as viscountess, wife and mother.

The newlyweds made their way down the aisle together, toward the door to the chapel. All their friends and family could hardly wait to congratulate them. Susan and George embraced them as they reached the end of the pews, and Susan planted tear-stained kisses on her cheeks.

"Darling, that was so beautiful," she said. "I could not be happier for the two of you."

George nodded, kissing the air beside Sophia's cheek after releasing his brother from a big embrace.

"Welcome to the family, dear sister," he said with a big smile.

Henry and Elizabeth were the last to greet their father and new stepmother. They each chose a parent and took their respective hands.

"It is hard to believe that you are our mother now," Henry said, grinning. "I do not believe we could ever ask for a better new mother than you."

Sophia smiled, embracing the boy.

"I am certainly the luckiest stepmother in all of England," she said.

The newlywed couple and their guests made the journey back to Rollins Manor, where Augusta had arranged the loveliest wedding breakfast. Julian looked perplexed, and Sophia had to bite her lip to keep from laughing. She had not been told for sure when Augusta visited the previous night. But she was certain deep down that her new mother-in-law had planned the celebration in secret.

She waited for the dowager to approach and kiss her son on the cheek.

"Forgive the secrecy, darling," she said. "But I wanted this to be a surprise. Sophia and I have reconciled, and I wanted this to be my wedding present to you, to show you that I understand how wrong I was about your marriage to her."

Julian looked stunned. He turned to Sophia for confirmation, which she gave with a sweet smile and gentle kiss on the lips.

"It is true, darling," she said.

Julian's face lit up, and he took both women into his arms.

"You do not know how happy that makes me," he said, kissing Sophia on the lips and his mother on the cheek.

Sophia laughed.

"I know how happy it would have made me if you had gotten those kisses backward," she said.

Julian tried to glower at her, but his lips trembled until he was howling with laughter.

"That would have been the talk of the town," he said.

"Speaking of gossip," Augusta said with a conspiratorial look. "It has been said that Lady Irene is now being courted by another nobleman. A marquess of notable wealth, I understand."

The desire to laugh was evident in Augusta's expression, causing Sophia to begin giggling.

"Well, I hope she finds happiness," she said.

Julian rolled his eyes in such a humorous way that even his mother burst out laughing.

"As long as she can roll in her future husband's fortune, she will be in pure bliss," he said.

The three of them shared a laugh.

Extended Epilogue

Sophia sat in a rocking chair in a lavish nursery, cradling a small bundle in her arms. Little Lily Rollins was not yet two months old, and she was one of the most brilliant lights of Sophia's life. The infant, having just nursed, was waving a tiny fist in the air, staring at it with eyes that were still trying to focus as intently as her father stared at a complex business problem. The other two children, who felt as much like her own as little Lily was, were playing in the corner, keeping their voices low in case their new baby sister should fall asleep.

When Lily cooed loudly, however, both Henry and Elizabeth, now ten and eight, respectively, rushed over, whispering excitedly over the infant.

"She looks just like Sophia," Elizabeth said, brushing a thick tuft of honey colored hair from her forehead.

"She has Father's eyes," Henry said, pointing carefully at the little girl's eyes, which were still the blue of most newborn and infant babies. However, there was the faintest hint of green forming around the pupils, and Sophia imagined that her eyes would wind up the same piercing green as those of her father.

Sophia smiled at all three of her children, still amazed at how much her life had been enriched since the two oldest had entered her life. Even after a whole year, she still awoke each morning, struggling to believe how fortunate and wealthy she was, both financially and most importantly, emotionally.

"There they are," Julian said, stepping inside the nursery of their new London townhouse. "The four people I love most in the whole world."

Sophia smiled up at him as he stared at them with eyes overflowing with adoration for the children and her. Henry and Elizabeth left their little sister to wrap themselves around their father's waist.

"Good day, Papa," Elizabeth said, beaming up at her father.

"We missed you," Henry said, squeezing Julian tightly.

Julian laughed, returning his oldest children's embrace.

"Good day, my precious ones," he said, kissing the tops of their heads. "And I have missed you all, as well."

As he made his way to Sophia, she giggled.

"It has only been a couple of hours," she said as he knelt down in front of her.

Julian glanced up at her as he stroked the soft silk that was Lily's hair.

"It might as well have been a couple of days," he said, staring down at the little miracle in his wife's arms. He radiated pride as he looked at all their children, his smile one that only devoted fathers and husbands knew. Then, he moved toward Sophia and placed a sweet kiss on her lips. Their eyes met, much like they first did one year prior, and the love shared in their stare filled Sophia with the same gratitude she saw reflected in his eyes. They had created the most beautiful family, and Sophia knew she could never be more blessed.

"May I hold her?" he asked, looking once again at the tiny little girl.

Sophia giggled, playfully shaking her head.

"How dare you ask to hold your infant daughter, Lord Rollins?" she said. "You are lucky I do not have you caned."

Julian laughed. Sophia was reminded of how hollow and joyless his laughter had sounded when she first met him. Now, it sounded as though there was music in it, radiating happiness all throughout the room. Apart from her children's voices, Sophia thought it was her favorite sound in all the world.

"Heavens, whatever was I thinking?" he asked, winking at the older children. "Shall I inform the authorities myself?"

Everyone laughed as Sophia shook her head.

"Not today," she said, gently offering the infant to her father. "Perhaps tomorrow."

Julian grinned, nodding in agreement.

"I shall take that deal," he said as he took Lily from her. Immediately, his face brightened, and he smiled down at her. As he began murmuring to his youngest daughter, there was a knock on the open door. They all turned to see Augusta in the doorway with one hand on her chest and a warm smile on her face.

"May I see her?" she asked, looking at Sophia with hopeful eyes.

Sophia motioned her inside eagerly, nodding and pointing to Julian.

"If you can pry her from her father's hands," she said with another giggle.

Augusta approached her son, who proudly held out his daughter to his mother. Augusta took her as delicately as Julian had, her warm smile spreading.

"Oh, what a beautiful little darling," she cooed softly. "I foresee a great deal of grandmotherly spoiling in your future, precious girl."

The other children let out cries of the most exaggerated indignation.

"What about us, Grandmother?" Elizabeth asked, pretending to whine as she struggled not to giggle.

Julian grabbed one of the dowager's hands, looking up at her with exaggeratedly wide eyes.

"Yes, what about us?" he asked, sticking out his bottom lip. "Are we not precious and beautiful, too?"

Augusta laughed and, much like her son's, the sound was far more genuine and carefree than it had once been.

"Oh, heavens, whatever shall I do with all three of you?" she asked.

Julian grinned at his mother, holding out his hands in a silent gesture to request to hold his daughter again.

"I am certain that you will find some way to manage, Mother," he said, laughing once more as he took back Lily and kissed his mother on both her cheeks. The relationship between the three of them had improved almost immediately after the wedding, and the dowager doted on her son and daughter-in-law almost as much as she did the children. It truly was every bit the happy family dynamic for which Sophia had hoped on the day that Augusta had apologized to her.

"Where is my new niece?" came another familiar voice from the doorway.

"Lucy," Sophia said before Julian and the dowager stepped aside to reveal her younger sister.

"You can hold your new niece after I get to hold my new granddaughter," Caroline said with a musical laugh.

Sophia grinned, waving the two women who were the reason her new, happy life was possible, to come toward her.

"Everyone shall get a turn with our dear little one," she said. "Right now, it is Augusta's turn. Tell me, how do you like your new home?"

Lucy's eyes lit up and she threw her arms around her older sister.

"Sophie, it is beautiful," she said. "We just got ourselves settled in, and it is magnificent. You must come see it soon. It overlooks the Thames River, and at night, we can see nothing but stars and the moon reflected off its waters. And on nights when the wind is a little more intense, we can hear it creating small waves in the river. I cannot thank you enough for such kindness, Sister."

Sophia gave her sister a gentle head shake.

"Do not thank me, Sister," she said. "If not for Julian, that would not have been possible. It is he whom you should be thanking."

Julian held up his hands, even as Lucy lunged at him for a hug.

"I shall accept no such credit," he said. "I did nothing more than take care of my family. The two of you deserve it, and my Sophia deserves to know that those she loves most are going to be well taken care of."

Caroline joined her daughter in embracing Julian.

"You can be as modest and humble as you like, Julian," she said. "But you will never know just how much this truly means to us. You helped me to get well again, and now both my daughters and I live a nice, comfortable life because of you. Thank you, darling."

Sophia giggled again as Julian blushed. But the smile on his face told her that he was proud to have made such a difference in their lives. She was proud of him too, and she could not have been more grateful that she had met him.

"It is my honour and pleasure to help you, Caroline," Julian said, returning the women's affectionate embrace.

"Are we late?" Susan said from the doorway.

Julian whirled around, giving his sister in law a humorously confused expression.

"Late for the birth?" he asked. "Only by a few weeks."

Susan and George both burst out laughing, embracing first Julian and then Augusta. They exchanged warm greetings with Caroline and Lucy, giving Henry and Elizabeth loving kisses atop their heads. Then, they approached the chair where Sophia sat with Lily, holding packages out toward them.

"We were beside ourselves, waiting for the chance to bring these to you together," George said. "I was away on business for a couple of weeks, and it has been driving both Susan and me mad."

Sophia accepted cheek kisses from both of them, glancing up at Julian, who was already moving to take the packages from his brother and sister-in-law.

"I shall take those," he said, holding them close to his chest and pretending to hoard them. "Only I cannot say that Lily will get to open any."

There was more laughter. Elizabeth and Henry, ever observant, burst through the cluster of adults.

"Did you bring something for us?" Elizabeth asked.

Henry gently nudged his sister out of the way, giving her an impish smile as he did so.

"Me first," he said with a fit of playful laughter.

George kissed little Lily atop her head and stroked her tiny pink cheek before turning back to the older children.

"Of course, I brought you something, as well," he said. "Did you think that I would leave my first niece and nephew out of the gift circle?"

Elizabeth shook her head, giggling.

"No, Uncle George," she said. "We were only teasing."

George gasped, looking shocked.

"Oh, you were?" he asked. "Well, then, I suppose we could just give them all to Lily."

The children shrieked, causing all the older people in the room to laugh again.

"May we please have our presents?" Henry asked.

Julian handed them the packages that George delegated to the older children. Then, he took the remaining ones over to Sophia, kneeling down beside her on the floor as he had when he kissed her.

"Would you like me to help you open them, darling?" he asked.

Sophia playfully snatched a box and tried to make a sour face through her smile.

"I believe you might steal them," she said, unable to hold back more laughter.

With all their loved ones watching, they opened the three small packages. Inside one, there was a brand-new doll with the loveliest pink satin dress, dark brown hair and bright green eyes. Next, there was a soft yellow blanket they could use when they took Lily on walks in her stroller. And lastly, there was the most beautiful blue silk dress and matching slipper and bonnet.

"Her very first dress, which is the same shade as her mother's eyes," Susan said, beaming at Sophia.

Sophia looked at the outfit again, noticing that Susan was right. It was identical to the blue of her eyes. George and Susan must have gone to great lengths to make such a match, and her eyes filled with tears.

"These are absolutely wonderful," she said. "Thank you both."

Susan gave her another hug, while George stepped up behind Julian. He pulled him to the side, but not so far that Sophia could not hear what the brothers were saying.

"Julian, I am thrilled that you have found yourself such a wonderful life," he said. "Congratulations, dear brother. I cannot think of anyone who deserves this happiness more than you, the children and Sophia."

Julian grinned at his brother, clapping him on the back.

"Thank you, George," he said. "I might not have dared to try for such happiness, had it not been for your words."

George shrugged, preparing to say something else. But Sophia tuned it out, not wanting to continue eavesdropping on the private moment between brothers.

With laughter and love filling the room, Sophia felt as though she was truly at home. Even her father's presence could be felt, watching over her and little Lily as they sat surrounded by the people who adored them most in the world. Julian finally rejoined his wife, and the two of them sat watching their loved ones enjoying the company of one another. Sophia smiled up at her husband, who leaned down and gave her another gentle kiss.

"Everything in life that was meant to break us led to this moment, you know," Julian said.

Sophia beamed at him, thrilled to hear him say those words.

"I am so proud of you, darling," she said, kissing him again. "And I could not agree more."

Julian gave her a proud grin and a nod.

"I am proud of me, as well," he teased. "And I am proud of both of us. We have the strongest love of anyone in all of England. And I could not be more grateful."

Sophia nodded, nestling her head against her husband's side.

"Nor could I, my love," she said.

The End

Printed in Great Britain
by Amazon